Sharia Law Shakespeare

Feridon Rashidi

Published by New Generation Publishing in 2017

Copyright © Feridon Rashidi 2017

First Edition

www.newgeneration-publishing.com

New Generation Publishing

Dedicated to the memory of the great Iranian humanist playwright, novelist, and short story writer, Gholam-Hossein Sa`edi, who was imprisoned and tortured under the Shah's regime, and was sent into exile by the regime of the mollahs. This story is partly inspired by his life and work.

From this wasteland inhabited by Iranians, Turks, and Arabs
Will emerge a motley grotesque race.
It will be neither Iranian, nor Turk, nor Arab,
Who will talk to one another in gibberish.
They will cunningly disguise their true motives,
And will vie with one another in surrendering to their belligerent enemies.
The virtue of loyalty will vanish from this land,
In which people will take pleasure in tormenting one another, in words and in deeds.
They will trample on their humanity and spill blood to gain riches.
Those times will be the ugliest in our history.
By concealing themselves behind the conquering religion,
They will be ruthless in harming others to gain their own benefits.

Adapted for our times from the epic of *Shahnameh*
(Ferdowsi, AD 940-1020)

Contents

COMEDY

My arrival on the scene of this world was accompanied by farcical Islamic dramas. It was the holy month of *Moharram* and the entire village that day had thronged to the little square in front of the mosque, opposite our house, to watch what I call the Islamic version of opera called *ta'zieh*, during which the village men act out the tale of Imam Hossein's martyrdom. Later on in my life my mother told me the actors and the villagers made such a clamour in the neighbourhood and the square that I kept crying non-stop and waking up with a start. Everybody was yelling and running around to make sure they could find a place with a good view to settle and watch the religious show. The blare of trumpets, the chanting of the actors, the braying of donkeys, the hysterical screeching of women, the ear-splitting howling of babies and children, the bleating of sheep and the squabbling of young men over young women went on and on. The whole village had turned into a deafening and grotesque carnival.

After the *ta'zieh* a procession of cleaver-brandishing men, draped in shrouds, marched into the square, slashing their foreheads with cleavers. This was then followed by a longer procession of black-clad, self-flagellating men. All the children, young and old, were freaked out watching these absurd, devilish dramas.

A year after my birth I was taken to a more comic drama than the gruesome ones described above. This was the Shiite festival of *Omar-koshaan*, when the scarecrowlike effigy of Omar, the first Islamic caliph, is burnt, spat at and insulted by the lunatic crowd of

1

villagers. Later on, when I was a bit older, this festival always made me laugh as it had far more of a carnival atmosphere, albeit poisoned with religious hatred.

As I grew older I saw more and more the humorous side of these supposedly solemn ceremonies. What made me laugh a lot secretly with my brother and friends, while sitting in masques and *tekiehs*, was that all the opium junkies, gamblers, alcoholics, pimps, child-molesters, knife-fighters and all types of louts put on religious masks, joining these shows and festivals. Some of these men even acted as organisers who directed the shows, bullied the folk around and chanted dirges for the Prince of the Martyrs, Imam Hossein.

Having inherited a good sense of humour from my paternal grandmother, who never took Islamic rituals seriously, always poking fun at religious folk and their pomposity, I soon came to make fun of these hypocrites by mimicking them whenever I found the opportunity. My brother and sisters laughed a lot watching me ridiculing these people, my relatives and strangers alike. Among the many acts that made them laugh helplessly was when I wound a piece of white cloth round my head, making it look like a turban, and threw one of my grandmother's *chadors* over my shoulder as if it was an *abaa*. I would then sing, dance, and wriggle my bum, looking like a foolish mollah. My sister and cousins would fall about with laughter.

Even behind all that façade of violence that went on in the village and downtown Tehran, I always saw the hilarity and foolhardiness of my neighbours and relatives. All wedding ceremonies that took place in the decorated courtyards in our lane invariably ended up in squabbles and brawls between rival relatives. Most funerals ended up in score-settling among the heirs of the departed one, who fought one another over the inheritance immediately after the burial of the deceased. Young boys, terrified and swathed in loincloths, gave slip to the razor-brandishing barber before the circumcision ceremonies got going, and ran off and hid where no one could find them easily. Women tore one another's clothes into shreds in the lanes over their husbands' affairs with their prettier rivals. Child-molesters in bicycle-hire shops fondled young boys under the pretence of teaching them how to ride a bicycle. Street-pedlars were harassed by ragamuffins who stole the goods piled up on their donkeys. Pigeon-fanciers spent all day watching their pigeons soar in the skies talking about nothing but their pretty birds. Lovesick, skinny young men lurked all day long in the streets and lanes to catch a glimpse of young ladies who were in love with other, more promising young men.

Throughout my childhood in the poor quarters of downtown Tehran the word theatre was a mystery to me. What really fired my imagination and kindled my interest in theatre was a marionette show. When, for the first time, an itinerant *morshed* set up his booth in our lane a whole new world was opened up to my eager eyes. As we sat on the dusty ground, watching the marionettes whose adventures were described by the morshed. I was lost in a magical world of princes, princesses, heroes, and wicked witches.

When my father took me, for the first time, to a teahouse in which a storyteller told the stories from the *Shahnameh*, my imagination was stretched even more by these wonderful mythological tales. I was about ten when my best friend, Majeed, introduced me to serialised Persian tales in a magazine called *Sepeed-o-Siyah*. The ill-

3

tempered owner of a dingy little corner shop, which smelled of peppermint sweets, sewed a large number of back issues of this magazine together which he rented out for a *gheran* a week. Majeed and I put our *shahi* coins together and rented these bulky tomes, sitting in the shade of the oleander bush in our small courtyard and reading the stories with relish to each other.

I was about sixteen when, roaming with my brother, Nasser, in the fashionable Lalezaar district, I watched a show in the Sa'di Theatre for the first time.

"If this is what *tiarte* is all about," I said to Nasser, when out in the street, "for the whole of our lives we've either been watching *tiartes* all around us or have been taking part in many without knowing it."

"You're right," Nasser said, grinning. "We've been a good audience, and good actors, too."

It was as if a door to a new room had been opened to me. From then on I saved my pocket money and, whenever I could, I would see a play in the various theatres in Lalezaar, accompanied by my brother and some close friends.

Soon I discovered a small theatre workshop in central Tehran, run by a bunch of playwrights, actors, and actresses. I immediately became a member and my life started to change.

"You know, Nasser," I said one day to my brother as we sauntered aimlessly in Estanbol Avenue, "I'm thinking of trying my hand at writing a play myself."

"What about?"

"Well," I said, "about some of the many dramas that have been going on around us in our lives."

"I reckon you're right," Nasser said. "There are plenty of them and some of them are very funny, too."

4

I did not, however, manage to write something significant till rather later in my life because of the many social and political upheavals. After the Anglo-American *coup d'état* that overthrew the democratically elected government of Dr Mosaddegh, my life was thrown into turmoil. A very different kind of drama in my own life and the lives of people of my generation started after this most shameful treachery in our history since the invasion of the Arabs, fourteen centuries ago. The return of the Pahlavi regime to power created the impetus for me to write several plays, some of which were staged in both old and modern theatres. Soon my highly social and political plays put me at loggerheads with the infernal secret police of the Shah – SAVAC. Not heeding the first polite warnings of SAVAC, soon I was thrown into the notorious Evin prison. As I was not one who would ever betray my friends and comrades under humiliation and torture, they released me after a year. Once out of prison, I resumed my writing of plays, short stories, and novels.

A number of years before the upheavals of 1979, I produced Shakespeare's *Othello* in the Department of Dramatic Arts at the University of Tehran. For a playwright and director with a group of enthusiastic amateur and professional actors the response we received from our audiences was quite encouraging. Drama being my main passion, I soon formed a new small amateur theatre troupe, rented a modest studio down in the Lalezaar district and put on some Iranian and foreign plays.

The cataclysmic events after the Revolution changed everything beyond our expectations. All aspects of our lives and culture came to be controlled by the Islamic

Republic regime. Every work of imagination had to be scrutinised by a bunch of bearded mollahs crawling out of villages and hamlets forgotten by time, who had crept into rooms in the Ministry of Islamic Culture and Guidance. When a work of art – a novel, play, painting, music, etc. – emerged from the in-depth examination of those know-it-alls, it became completely distorted and turned into the most freakish abomination, resembling anything but a work of art.

After June 1980 the regime started to implement, in a most barbaric fashion, its so-called Cultural Revolution, Islamising all subjects in the universities by purging non-Islamic lecturers and professors and propping up Muslim ones. Soon after this, the regime of ayatollahs turned their attention to the arts. Working diligently, the regime put an end to all the professional and amateur theatre troupes all over the country. A brief communiqué from the *Monkaraat* Unit banned professional theatre companies from producing plays of any kind.

This unit, which had nothing to do with cultural and artistic activities, was an organ of inquisition, created by the Islamic regime, whose task was to poke its nose into people's way of life and beliefs to root out all non-Islamic practices and ideas. Hordes of bearded thugs from the *Monkaraat* assiduously attacked the small theatres, beat up the actors, smashed the stage props, and even kicked and punched the bewildered audience, who had just wanted to enjoy a bit of culture. As a result, amateur theatre troupes were forced out of their activities and stopped producing plays altogether. Many of the directors and actors left Iran for good and those such as myself, who stayed in the country, kept a low profile by getting on with our daily lives.

Being aware of the immense power of drama, the lackeys of the regime soon allowed a handful of plays to be produced if they complied strictly with the law of the land – Sharia Law. Islamic dramas began to mushroom in the former theatres in and around central Tehran. These religious dramas were only popular with the faithful, who sat in the halls, weeping and beating their chests as if they were watching a *ta'zieh* in a village square or a *tekieh* set up in a house in a lane. Having wept to their hearts' content, these folk would leave the theatre satisfied.

Producing plays being my passion, I thought perhaps the Islamic regime would be more cooperative and understanding if I put to them my intention of directing one of Shakespeare's tragedies. The choice of tragedy was deliberate on my part, as Shakespearian comedy, or any other comedy for that matter, had no place whatsoever in an Islamic society. A sense of humour, when spiced with subtle irony, in the way that has existed in Western cultural tradition since the golden age of the Greeks, would never have a place in a deeply Islamic country, let alone one ruled by Sharia Law. What could, therefore, be more fitting than the tragedy of *Othello*, whose main protagonist was a brave Moorish general who trusted his friends and was madly in love with his white-skinned, blonde wife? Having been betrayed by his wife with his trusted friend, at the end of the play Othello suffocates her in her bed and then, finding out that he had been tricked into committing this cruel deed by his closest friend, he thrusts a sword into himself. The mollahs would love the character because, having been, as he thinks, cuckolded, he kills his wife in the manner of a good Muslim man whose honour has been besmirched. A welcome perk of this play would be that it might make the good Muslim audience weep a little, thinking of their own fragility as wretched human beings – creatures of Allah who are nothing but a cesspit of chaotic emotions such as jealousy, rage, obsessive love, envy, avarice and much more!

*

One hot day in July of 1980 my journalist friend Amir and I, sick and tired of witnessing recent events, sat on a bench in the City Park in midtown Tehran to smoke and talk. Tehran's citizens were scurrying here and there like confused insects trying to run away from an imminent catastrophe.

"You know what, Amir?" I said.

"What?" Amir said, not particularly interested.

"I'm thinking of staging one of Shakespeare's tragedies in that place." I nodded towards the City Theatre outside which hung huge posters with slogans showing what an Islamic drama should look like.

"A Shakespearian tragedy in the City Theatre!" Amir laughed mockingly.

"Yes," I said. "What's wrong with that?"

"A lot of things, Behrouz."

"What? For example."

"Primo, a lot of Western plays cannot be staged in the Islamic Republic for having women in them who don't wear the Islamic hijab. Secondo, the regime pig-headedly disapproves of their non-Islamic content." Amir counted off his points on his fingers. "Tertio, all the plays should go along, to the letter, with the decrees of Sharia Law. An army of self-appointed mollahs and ayatollahs, each one of whom imagines he's an expert in some field of art, residing in the Ministry of Islamic Culture and Guidance, will swarm on the play like vermin, mangling it beyond recognition to make it look more Islamic."

"As if I didn't know that."

"If you know, then, why are you even thinking about it?"

"There's no harm in trying. We cannot deprive Tehran's people of the fruits of Western civilisation."

"But you know very well that the ayatollahs don't give a monkey's about the fruits of Western civilisation."

We sat there contemplating the beautiful City Theatre with its colourful mosaic patterns glistening in the sun.

"Which play do you have in mind, anyway?" Amir asked.

"*Othello*, of course."

"Er," Amir mumbled, "if you're so keen about this, that one seems a good one."

"Do you think you can help me do it? Do you remember those days of our youth and how many great plays we saw in that place, Amir?" I asked him.

"How can I forget all that, Behrouz?"

"Camus's *Caligula*, Chekhov's *The Seagull*, and many others," I said, sighing.

"Don't forget the brilliant works of the Iranian writers, such as Sa`edi, Saghiri, Khalaj, Raadi, and a few others that I don't remember."

"Those were the days, Amir," I said.

"Hmm," Amir repeated, "those were the days."

"You see," I said, "even if the Pahlavi regime did its best to suppress our freedoms, their flunkies lacked the intellectual capacity to censor all works of art."

"How could those men who worked in SAVAK see the hidden messages in novels, poems and short stories?" Amir agreed. "Those half-wit sons of whores were all

9

either orphans or picked up from the most depraved and deprived places in the country."

Around us sparrows twittered among the branches, chasing insects in the warm air.

"So," I said. "Shall we give it a go?"

"What?"

"Staging one of Shakespeare's tragedies, of course."

"You can count me in," Amir said, "even though my acting skills have gone a bit rusty." He then added, "I hope you realise that this is not going to be an easy ride."

"I know that I'll have to go through Seven Labours of *Rostam* to get the licence for this play."

"I wish you luck, mate."

"Do you think you can play the role of Othello for me?" I said after a bit of thought.

"Othello?"

"Yes, Othello."

"I think you have to find someone who looks a bit like him."

"Among all my friends, you seem to be the best candidate for the role," I said. "You're tall, barrel-chested, have a deep voice, a swarthy face and a manly moustache. All you need is to grow a beard."

"If I have to grow a beard," Amir said, "I will be out. I will do anything not to look like those motherfucker mollahs."

"All right, then," I said hastily to cool Amir's fiery temper. "With some skilful make-up you'll look the spitting image of the famous moor."

*

10

It took me a week to track down my old actor friends. Some of them agreed, albeit half-heartedly, to help me in my dramatic venture. I asked them to meet me, on a Friday, in my flat in midtown Tehran.

On the appointed day they came. Having gone through a lot of humiliation in the past two years, none of them seemed, at the start, to be optimistic about my project, but after some persuasion they finally agreed to play a part in the tragedy.

"As you know, Behrouz, we now all have families and day jobs," Goudarz reminded me.

"Yes, I know."

"We will have a crack at it only because we love drama," Jahaangir said. "But if we get beaten up, sworn at or accused of anti-Islamic activities, I'll kiss the theatre goodbye for good."

"Not to worry," I assured them all. "I'll make sure that will not happen."

"Have you found a place where we can practise?" Arezoo asked.

"A tailor friend of mine knows an abandoned tailor's workshop right opposite the American Embassy," I said. "He has agreed to let us use it for our rehearsals."

"Say the mollahs agree that the production of the play can go ahead," Goudarz joined in, "where are you intending to stage it?"

"The old Theatre Studio near Lalezaar, where we put on some of our plays years ago is now disused," I said. "I'll see if we can rent it for a while."

Soon after our meeting I wrote a polite letter to *Sheik-ol-eslam* Pashmeddin in the Ministry of Islamic Culture and Guidance who, after the revolution, had taken upon himself the job of the Culture Minister, becoming overnight a film and drama critic. He was the person responsible for the issuing of licences for films and plays. Having no time to waste, I managed to rent the old studio for a few months.

One Friday evening we all gathered in the deserted tailor's workshop to discuss to whom to allocate the roles. I handed each actor a copy of the script that I had written. All being familiar with the tragedy, we talked about the characters and agreed that the role of Othello would suit Amir best. Jahaangir, looking a bit devilish, accepted the role of Iago, Goudarz was happy to act as Cassio, while Arezoo agreed to be Desdemona, with Faraanak as Emilia, and Shahnaaz as Bianca. Each took a copy of the script home to read, memorise and act out the speeches spoken by their characters.

An old friend of mine who was a costume designer agreed to make the costumes.

Every Friday afternoon we met in the derelict workshop and I directed the rehearsals. We carried on with our practice while waiting for the licence to be issued. After several sessions we felt that we were ready to stage the play. Amir and I visited some second-hand shops in the Bazaar, from where we bought cheap furniture for the set and we bought some fabric from a mercer's shop. We all got together, as we had done in the old days, and decorated the studio. We used some of the furniture as stage props. From a dealer who rented out chairs for wedding ceremonies, I managed to get fifty chairs for the potential audience.

Fed up with chasing the cursed licence, I took the matter into my own hands and set off one day to the Ministry of Islamic Culture and Guidance. There were so many flustered-looking film-makers, artists, musicians and theatre directors, who had come to get hold of their licences, hurrying about in the corridors of the colossal building. After spending the whole day in the interminable labyrinths of the Ministry, being passed from one bearded clerk to another, I finally managed to obtain what I was after. I thrust the precious piece of paper into my jacket pocket and rushed out of the building before they could change their minds, telling me that there had been a blunder. Over the moon, I sat in a bus, ready to do my bit to civilise the Tehranis.

The Friday of the same week, when I arrived at the workshop, all my friends, garbed in their Shakespearian attire, were already there, standing or strutting up and down the stage, posing in their roles, and reciting their lines in dramatic manner. I stood still near the door of the small hall, looking at them. Every now and then they came out of their roles and cracked jokes and laughed. Noticing me standing there unusually quiet, they all stopped and regarded me curiously, sensing that I had something to tell them. I climbed up on to the stage and regarded them in silence.

"We won!" I shouted, pulling the piece of paper out of my pocket and waving it in the air like a hard-won trophy.

"What did we win?" Othello asked.

"The licence, the licence, the licence ..." I sang, clicking my fingers and jumping up and down like a clown.

"You're joking," Cassio said.

"You mean *the* licence," Iago corrected me.

They applauded me for my doggedness and began kissing and hugging each other.

"Didn't I tell you that I was capable of fooling these mollahs," I said, euphoric.

"Keep your voices down, all of you," Desdemona reminded us frantically, pointing to the door. "You know that these days walls have ears."

She was right, as I knew that any minute the flunkies of the regime could walk in to see what we were up to. I beckoned everyone to gather round me to listen to what was written in the licence.

"You see, guys," I said in a low voice, casting cautious glances at the door, "although these fools do their utmost to stop artists doing what they want freely, they are just a bunch of imbeciles who can easily be tricked by using their own language against them."

"Can you just read the damned thing to tell us what's in it?" Othello said.

"In the Name of Allah," I read, "a licence is granted to the Shahrzaad Amateur Theatre Troupe to stage the tragedy of Shakespeare written by the Queen Elizabeth's playwright, Othello."

"*Aye zeki!*" Othello burst into laughter, glancing round at everyone. "The tragedy of Shakespeare written by Othello!"

"Come on, Agha Othello," Iago said. "What did you expect from these mollahs?"

"They mean Othello written by Shakespeare, all right." I corrected the text.

Iago assumed a theatrical posture and recited one of his lines in the play:

> *When devils will the blackest sins put on,*
> *They do suggest at first with heavenly shows,*
> *As I do now.*

"No doubt this is a typing error by one of those pen-pushers in the Ministry," I said.

"Can we just get on with it, Agha Othello?" Desdemona insisted.

"All right, then," Othello said.

"They've demanded a few minor conditions," I went on, "none of which is really significant."

The actors looked at one another questioningly.

"*You advise me well,*" Cassio recited in a dramatic tone.

"Where's that line?" I asked.

"Act 2 Scene 3."

"Just wait a little," I said. "We're not rehearsing yet." I then carried on reading the rest of the licence: "In the production of the play the following criteria must be strictly observed. Condition One: you must refrain, at all costs, from using obscene words while acting.

"There are no obscene words in the play," Emilia said.

"That means no offensive words against Islamic morality," Iago explained. "Instead of me, for example, telling you, in Act 2 Scene 1, '*Come on, come on: you are pictures out of doors, bells in your parlours, wild cats in your kitchens, saints in your injuries, devils being offended, players in your housewifery, and housewives in your beds,*' I should tell you: '*players in your housewifery, and Maashallah in your beds!*'

"Condition Two," I read on, glaring at Iago. "Islamic hijab must be fully observed."

"Islamic hijab!" Desdemona echoed loudly in bewilderment. "In Shakespeare's tragedy!"

"Don't worry," I said. "Headscarves for female actors will do the job."

"That means when I'm alone with my husband in my home I should wear a detestable hijab!"

"*Baba jaan*, this is a drama, do you understand?" I told her. "The director's hands are free to adapt it to different ages and social conditions in human history."

"You're right in that," Desdemona said. "Adapting it to the barbaric ages of fourteen centuries ago in the Arabian Peninsula!"

"There will be, in all likelihood, some fanatical Muslims with their wives and husbands in the audience," I pointed out. "We're living in very different times now. We cannot go against the religious sensibilities of large number of Tehranis. For them a woman must cover herself, no matter who she is and what role she plays!"

Furious, Desdemona fell silent.

"Condition Three," I read. "The ideals of the Islamic Republic must be wholly respected."

"Brilliant!" Othello said, laughing and shaking his head. "This tops all the absurdities."

"For heaven's sake," I said. "If you can be patient a bit I'll explain it all."

"What do they mean by that, I wonder?" Cassio asked.

"They've explained it all here," I said. "For example, Iago must be portrayed as an anti-revolutionary who plots a *coup-d'état* against the Islamic Republic."

"Me?" Iago said, pointing to himself. "Smashing! That's all I need now, to be arrested tomorrow in the street as an anti-Islamic communist and be taken to the Revolutionary Committee!"

"No one will recognise you in the streets," I said. "You'll look very different on the stage when you wear your costume and make-up."

"People will know who I am," Iago protested. "Isn't my name going to be splashed on all the publicity posters?"

"If that's what worries you," I assured him, "we'll invent a different name for you. Are you happy now?"

Iago gazed at the floor.

"Cassio must be portrayed as a young revolutionary guard who is devoted unconditionally to our beloved leader Imam Khomeini," I read. "He must be shown as a pious Muslim who, thanks to conspiracies against him by the enemies of Islam, suffers tragically and becomes a martyr to the ideals of the revolution."

"He's portrayed, more or less, like this in the play," Cassio pointed out. "A good loyal soldier to the king and his general, Othello."

"That's it, then," Iago chipped in. "Soon Cassio's virtues as a martyr-to-be will be trumpeted in pomp and circumstance in the regime's media."

"Will you just shut up all of you and listen to the rest of the conditions," Desdemona yelled.

"Condition Four: Half of the proceeds from the ticket sales must be given as charity to the Martyrs' Foundation and the Centre for Islamic Ideology and Art."

"What proceeds?" Othello flared up, outraged.

"They'll do the accounting themselves," I said, looking at my watch and throwing anxious glances at the door. "You see, guys, you should not trouble yourselves too much with these niggling issues. We've been working hard to get this play off the ground and let's not get bogged down over these petty concerns. We don't have much time. In one hour's time the Minister of Islamic Guidance, *Hojjat-ol-eslam Sayyed* Pashmeddin, a representative from the headquarters of the Cultural Revolution, and an expert on artistic matters, will come here. We should get ready before their arrival."

"Here." Out of a gunnysack crammed with Islamic costumes, I pulled two black *chadors* and two black headscarves and handed them over to Desdemona and Emilia. "Put them on, please."

"You mean I'm going to look like one of those ravenlike *Hezbollahi* sisters!" Desdemona objected, snatching the items from me. She then turned to Emilia. "Do you think we should put them on, Emilia?"

"I'll wear whatever outfits you wear," Emilia replied, resigned to all this ludicrousness.

Albeit grudgingly, they put on the Islamic garments. They then pulled their scarves down to their faces, veiled themselves under the black *chadors* and began walking slowly round the stage, dragging their feet like women mourners in a *ta'zieh*, beating their chests and wailing mournfully:

> *Oh, you darling son of Fatemeh,*
> *I beseech you do not go to the battle,*
> *I beg you don't rush to your death,*
> *I beg you don't rush to your death.*

I sat there and watched them in despair. Iago accompanied the mourners of martyred Imam Hossein by beating his head rhythmically and weeping copiously. Cassio laughed hysterically, slapping his knee. Othello joined in by unsheathing his wooden sword and charging at Iago and Cassio in the manner of Shemr-ebn-e-Zeljoshan who, fourteen centuries ago, cut off the head of Imam Hossein, the grandson of the Prophet, in the Battle of Karbala.

"Sound the kettledrums and trumpets," Othello roared like Shemr in the heat of the battle, "to strike fear in the hearts of our mortal enemies."

"I didn't expect *you* to behave like this, *Jenaab*-e Othello," I said, at the end of my tether.

"All right, then," Othello said, coming out of Shemr's character. "What costume am *I* supposed to wear?"

"As you're an army general and a Muslim revolutionary," I told him, "you should wear a long robe."

Othello walked to the costume rack, found something resembling an Arabic robe and slipped it on.

"Now I can chop off anybody's head who dares to question my military prowess," he cried, throwing one flap of the robe over his left shoulder. He took on a warlike attitude, brandishing his sword.

"You can do whatever you like as long as you don't grumble," I told him.

"Excuse me, Agha Director," Iago asked politely. "Any idea as to what I should wear?"

"For the time being, you remain in your own clothes until I find a costume that suits your part."

"The truth is that, Iago, my friend," Cassio said, teasingly, "a costume cannot conceal what you really are – an anti-revolutionary who everyone can easily spot."

"Now you've the nerve to frame me up, you son of a gun," Iago said, delivering a kick to Cassio's backside.

*

Once everyone was ready, I told them to stand apart from each other somewhere on the stage and practise acting in their new costumes while I consulted my script to find the relevant acts to rehearse.

"Listen, everyone." I called for their attention. "We're going to practise from the middle of Act 3, Scene 3."

I told Othello and Iago to stand at the end of the stage and asked Emilia, Cassio and Desdemona to start from where the two friends enter the scene where Emilia is talking to Desdemona and Cassio. Emilia assumed her pose.

"*Madam, here comes my lord.*"

"*Madam …*" Cassio said.

"No, no, no," I interrupted Cassio. "You must not talk to Desdemona in the same tone as that of Emilia who talks like a lady-in-waiting. You should talk in a manly voice, respectfully, while lowering your eyes."

"*Madam, I'll take my leave*," Cassio said, more like a soldier.

"*Why, stay and hear me speak.*"

"*Madam, not now: I'm very ill at ease, unfit for mine own purposes.*"

"*Well, do your discretion.*"

"You now leave the stage, Cassio," I told him and asked Othello and Iago to enter precisely at the moment when Cassio was about to leave the scene.

"*Ha, I like not that*," Iago said, turning his head like a man who has suspected something shameful is going on.

"*What dost thou say?*" Othello asked.

"*Nothing, my lord; or if I know not what,*" Iago replied.

"Listen, Iago," I cut in. "There should be a pause between *or if* and *I know not what*."

"*Nothing, my lord, or if –*" Iago repeated, paused a little and went on, "*I know not what.*"

"*Was not that Cassio parted from my wife?*" Othello asked.

"If you could say this bit in the voice of a husband who's extremely mindful of the honour of his wife," I clarified for him, "it would have more dramatic effect."

"Not a clue as what you're talking about," Othello said.

"You're not only addressing Iago," I explained, "but also talking to a much wider audience; in other words, humanity."

"*Was not that Cassio parted from my wife?*" Othello said in the manner of a man whom jealousy has just begun to unsettle.

"*Cassio, my lord? No, sure, I cannot think it, /That he would steal away so guilty-like, /Seeing your coming,*" Iago replied.

"*I do believe 'twas he,*" Othello said.

*

Exactly at this moment the door of the hall was flung open and a thuggish-looking, heavily-bearded young man with a keffiyeh round his neck, pointing a Kalashnikov at us, leapt on to the stage.

"Where did he go?" he bawled.

All the actors froze, gazing at this neanderthal, who began to prowl about the stage.

"Where did he escape?" he screeched in his capon voice, walking to the costumes rack and poking the muzzle of his Kalashnikov in between the hangers.

"Who are you talking about, brother?" I said, recognising him as one of those dangerously fanatical revolutionary guards.

"The one who just fled," he said, sniffing every corner of the stage like a mongrel dog looking for offal.

"No one has escaped, my brother," I said calmly. "We're all here."

"Do you think I am a donkey?" he said. "I heard with my own ears that one brother said in a clever language he ran away from someone's wife, and the other brother said he believed it was him. What was his name?"

"No, brother," I said with a pacifying smile. "These brothers and sisters are practising scenes from a play."

With trembling hands, I showed him the script.

"Although I can read a bit," he brayed, not looking at the manuscript, which he knocked from my hand with the muzzle of his Kalashnikov, "we never read books like this. Anyway, *Haaj* Agha Pashmeddin and the brothers will be here any minute. We must make sure all is in order and safe before they arrive. "

Soon a thickly-built, bearded man, who looked like a ghoul dressed in black human clothes, walked into the hall, crept up to the stage, and began to examine all the nooks and crannies as quietly as a mute, beading his rosary in his hairy hands.

"Brothers and sister," the ghoul addressed the actors in his gruff voice, "stay apart from one another."

"*Yallah, yallah*," the guard barked. "All the sisters stand on one side and all the brothers on the other side." He glared at the actors. "Look at them; they're bunching together as if they're sitting around their auntie's *korsi*," he mocked.

Hearing this bogeyman growling again, Emilia and Desdemona huddled together like terrified little girls on one side of the stage. Othello, Cassio and Iago stood on the other side, dumbfounded.

The ghoul, after asking me to button up my shirt to my neck, walked to the guard, whispered something in his ear and both left the hall.

As soon as they were out, all the actors circled me, angrily demanding some explanation.

"Can you tell us what's going on?" they asked noisily.

"If you can be patient for a bit," I told them calmly, "all will soon become clear."

Within a minute or so Minister Sayyed Pashmeddin, a stocky, fat-bellied mollah in a black turban and camel-hair *abaa*, Ostaad Safihollah, a scraggy man with a pencil moustache and with his white shirt buttoned up to the throat, hugging a bundle of documents, Ostaad Honarkhor, a bespectacled, bald, nervy man clutching a briefcase, and a babuinalike woman, veiled from head to foot in a black *chador* from the Zainab Sisterhood stepped into the hall. The minister lifted his *abaa* and gingerly climbed up the steps on to the stage, with his retinue trailing behind him. Once on the stage, he stood still and scanned the actors and actresses, beading his rosary with his two hands, which he rested on his enormous belly. His companions lined up respectfully behind him.

"*Salaam aleikom*," the minister greeted the actors in his guttural, pompous voice.

"*Salaam aleikom, Hazrat-e Hojjat-ol-eslam*," I greeted the minister with exaggerated respect. "You are most welcome. Please be kind enough to take a seat."

I hurried to the three chairs on the left side of the stage, directing the guests to their seats. The minister led the way across the stage with his ponderous gait, followed by his two expert confederates. He took his time to settle down in the middle chair, wrapped himself up in his *abaa*, and arranged his turban on his head. The two officials seated themselves on the two chairs placed beside him. The revolutionary guard, gripping his Kalashnikov like a hungry man his food, hung about the door. The Zainab Sister stood beside him, pinching the hem of her chador under her chin. Both kept ogling the female actors.

"*Jenaab-e Hojjat-ol-eslam-e-val-moslemin* and the honourable ostaads," I addressed them with reverence, "thank you for obliging us by taking the trouble of visiting this cultural centre…"

I was cut short by the Zainab Sister's shrill voice.

"This is not the proper way to wear your hijabs, you hussies," she cawed, scuttling towards Desdemona. "Push that lock of hair under your headdress." She then turned to Emilia and said, "Yours is even more disgraceful and unislamic." Violently, she pulled Emilia's headdress down to her eyebrows. Next, she grabbed the bottom of their chadors, pulled them up roughly, examined their legs and ordered them to wear proper socks and cover their legs up.

"It's as if they've forgotten the pressure of the tombstone and the deadly bludgeons of angels *Nakir* and *Monker* in the first minutes in the grave," the Zainab Sister squealed, eyeing the female actors as if they were a couple of whores.

"Please, sister." Sayyed Pashmeddin had to keep her on a tight leash. "Let everyone sit till we decide what to say and do next." He then turned to the actors. "Please be seated, brothers and sisters."

I made a dash across the stage to the costume rack, found two pieces of cloth and threw them on Desdemona and Emilia's legs.

"Yes, it's very kind of you to have troubled yourself to come to this cultural centre." I grovelled before the officials. "We're all very grateful."

"I'm the one who should thank you," Sayyed Pashmeddin spoke with a drawl, twiddling his rosary between his chubby fingers similar to those of a man who cleans sewers, "for inviting a humble mollah such as me to your cultural centre. *Inshallah,* whatever our artist brothers

24

do in centres like this will serve the ideals of our Islamic revolution."

"*Jenaab-e Hojjat-ol-eslam*," Ostaad Safihollah lisped in his heavy Esfehani accent after standing up and fidgeting with his baggy jacket. "These young brothers and sisters are upstanding, devout Muslim actors who are about to stage a great play to promote the revolutionary ideals of the Islamic Republic. They have invited your eminence to benefit from your fathomless fount of knowledge and be guided by you in the straight path of Islam."

"I myself, of course, am in need of much enlightenment and guidance," Sayyed Pashmeddin drawled, feigning humility. "I will do what I possibly can not to withhold what paltry knowledge I have from sharing with my young fellow Muslims."

Next to speak was Ostaad Honarkhor, who stood up and arranged his oversized jacket.

"These brothers and sisters have accepted to adhere to all the criteria and principles of Islamic art in order to push forward our hallowed ideals." He expressed his views in his reedy voice with the self-importance of a complete know-it-all. "May I be bold enough to add to the fact that as we are endeavouring day and night to transmute Western science, technology and culture into Islamic ones, we must alter this form of art, namely drama, into an Islamic one as well." He turned to the minister and added, "*Inshallah*, under your fatherly and expert guidance our brothers and sisters will assist us to achieve these lofty goals."

I glanced at the actors. Seething with anger at what she was hearing, Desdemona covered her face in her hands. As she did so an unruly lock of her hair slipped out from under her headdress.

"Cover your hair, sister," the Zainab Sister squawked at her, revealing a cavernous mouth like the inside of a rotten pomegranate.

"They keep forgetting that they're living in an Islamic country," the revolutionary guard put in.

"I beg you, brother and sister." Ostaad Honarkhor stepped in. "Give a chance to Jenaab-e Minister to express his estimable views."

"Oy, you two," the Zainab Sister croaked at Desdemona and Emilia, "let's go to that back room so that our brothers can talk without you distracting them."

Desdemona and Emilia hesitated a bit, regarding the Zainab Sister like two little girls scared of an ugly, foul-tempered *efreeteh* in a black veil.

"What are you gawping at?" the veiled baboon shrieked, motioning them towards the back of the stage. "Get a move on."

Desdemona and Emilia looked at one another, lifted their unwieldy Islamic hijabs with their hands and followed the woman into the room.

"In the Name of Allah the Almighty," Sayyed Pashmeddin began languidly with an Arabic phrase, addressing the men present as if they were all sitting in a mosque. "May our blessings be upon our beloved Imam Khomeini, the commander-in-chief of our Islamic nation. May we also offer our benediction to our nation of martyr-begetters who has given us would-be martyred revolutionary guards who will be buried in their graves in blood-stained shrouds." As he droned on, he slowly lifted his right leg, propped it on the chair, hoisted himself up, shifted the other leg up, and scrunched up on the chair like

26

an aged gorilla. With an effort, he sluggishly raised himself up and rested his ample bottom on the backrest of the chair, as if it was a pulpit in a prayer-niche in a mosque. With great care he wrapped his *abaa* round his chunky person and went on fiddling with his rosary. Watching him, we all struggled to suppress our laughter.

"How fortunate we are to be among our Muslim brothers and sisters," he continued. "We are overcome by heavenly bliss. Let's hope that with the support of our artists dedicated to the Islamic Republic, we will achieve, to the envy of that Great Satan of America and his Zionist poodle, Israel, countless victories in our eternal battles of Islam against infidels, truth against untruth, true art against trash, civilisation against barbarism, and morality against immorality. Right at the outset I must emphasise that our imams, ayatollahs and mollahs have always put in and will go on putting in efforts of epic proportions in their combat against so-called Western civilisation. I have studied thoroughly all the great classic tomes written by our imams, ayatollahs and scholars on Islamic jurisprudence, logic, philosophy, psychology, medicine, geometry, trigonometry, arithmetic, astronomy, alchemy, astrology, mineralogy, zoology, botany, economy, and above all the twenty-four volumes of *The Oceans of Light* by Allaameh Majlessi in the Qom School of Theology. I also, when quite young, did some acting in *ta'ziehs* in my native village in the vicinity of the holy city of Qom. Endowed with an angelic voice since childhood, I was asked by the village elders to act in *ta'ziehs* during the holy months of *Moharram* and Ramadan. As I played the role of Hazrat Abbas, whose hands were chopped off by the cursed Shemr, all the men and women who watched me play and sing wept and beat their chests till a sizable number of them fainted. By acting thus for several years I managed to shoot two sparrows with a single stone: serving the martyred Imam Hossein and learning a thing or two about the art of *daraam.*"

"I'm delighted that his eminence knows so much about the art of drama." I hastened to praise and at the same time correct him.

"One can only do one's level best, brother director." Sayyed Pashmeddin chuckled modestly, tugging at his hennaed beard. "You may not be aware that our Muslim clerics dabble in everything under the sun. If an occasion demands, we sometimes even sing and dance to entertain our faithful brothers and sisters. One of the greatest imams in the past was quite an accomplished dancer, particularly in *samaa*, the ritual dance performed by Sufis."

The mollah stopped to draw breath after such lengthy windbaggery.

"What I am trying to preach here is for you to know that the art of *daraam*, among other things in our beloved Islam, is a religious duty, and like many others in our timeless, sacred Sharia Law, comes with its requirements. To give you an example of common everyday activity, the whole-body ablutions before daybreak, after a man has copulated with his wife, is a religious obligation and follows certain strict requirements. The art of *daraam*, like that of ablutions, has its own Islamic requirements that are based on three foundations, meaning three pillars.

"Three pillars?" Othello could not help echoing.

"Jenaab-e Minister means three principles," Ostaad Safihollah pitched in.

"Meaning three columns," Ostaad Honarkhor explained, keen to shed light on knotty theological concepts. "That's to say three supports, or three erections, if you prefer, in common parlance."

"Ostaad Honarkhor," the Minister snapped at him, "your opinions are most valued, but there is no need to labour the point to the point of absurdity."

"But of course," Ostaad Honarkhor agreed, lowering his head.

"I'm sure your holiness is referring to the unity of time, place, and action in drama," I politely pointed out.

"Listen, brother director," Sayyed Pashmeddin objected loudly, "these woolly, heretical notions come from the freethinkers in the West. How can we connect my small native village in Qom to Doomsday? There is only one unity and that is the unity of Allah and all the Muslims of the world!"

"I was only referring to the guidelines established by Aristotle," I explained.

"Who is Aris … what?" Sayyed Pashmeddin asked.

"Arabs called this Greek philosopher Arastaataalis," Ostaad Safihollah rushed to clarify.

"Aha, Arastaataalis," Sayyed Pashmeddin echoed. "Why didn't you say his name in Arabic? You know our Muslim scholars translated and studied all his works in Arabic. Where has he talked about such preposterous ideas, if you don't mind me asking?"

"In his book called *Poetics*," I said.

"Poe … what?"

"Haaj Agha," Ostaad Honarkhor poked his nose in again, "our brother means *Al-Bootighaa*."

"*Baleh, baleh*, I know now," Sayyed Pashmeddin said. "I studied that book in Arabic when I was a seminarian in the Qom School of Islamic Theology. From what I can recall, this Greek philosopher discoursed at length about the astrolabe, astronomy, and logic. His ideas belong to the materialistic school of philosophy, therefore are ungodly and non-Islamic. When was this book written?"

"Long before Jesus was born," Othello dared to answer.

"As the time of the writing of this book is before our beloved Islam," Sayyed Pashmeddin was quick to make things clear, "therefore it falls into the category of harmful books for our Islamic nation and ideology and therefore it is against our all-encompassing Sharia Law and any reference to it would be punishable severely by our laws."

"I wonder if you could enlighten us about those three foundations of Islamic art," I ventured to remind him; otherwise he would prattle on with his favourite gibberish.

"I was just about to come to my sermon on that subject," Sayyed Pashmeddin said, not happy about being cut short. "As I was saying, when we are dealing with Islamic *daraam* three principles must be obeyed. First and foremost, our *daraam,* just like our Islamic revolution, must be exported to the entire globe. For this reason our nation, following the tradition of Muslims in our glorious past, must be ready to shed their blood, sacrifice their young and give up everything they have, so that the colossal tree of the Islamic Republic will be laden with the fruits of our faith. In order to attain this sublime moral goal everybody must be ready and alert, at all times, to come out to the streets and shout against America, the Great Satan. As you know, our venerated Imam Khomeini called all of us a 'permanently-on-the-stage-nation'. This, if you can get the drift of what I am trying to make you understand from my preaching, means that we are never ourselves in our private lives. We are constantly taking part in this eternal *daraam* to keep the faith alive and kicking."

"And the second principle of Islamic drama?" I had to chip in as he was again going off the point with his hogwash.

"By the second foundation I mean that every individual must belong to *Hezbollah* so that he or she will be permanently on guard to pay his debt to our Islamic Revolution. By paying his debt, I mean to help us find every single man and woman who plots against our great revolution. These *Hezbollahi* young men and women have the unenviable burden of keeping our society uncontaminated from all these noxious human weeds that try to kill off the yet feeble saplings of our Islamic movement. Once these traitors are ferreted out of their wretched holes, they will be punished according to our Sharia Law, depending on the severity of their crimes – immediate hanging, lashing or stoning to death. All these castigations will be the best lessons for those who ever dare to contemplate going against our cherished ideology. These chastisements are nothing compared to what these sinners will have to suffer in Hell after their death till the Day of Judgement."

"And the third ..." I was about to remind him of the third principle when he cut me short.

"That's what I was coming to, if you will listen and show some respect."

"I beg your pardon, Jenab-e Minister," I mumbled.

"The third pillar is about the penitents, and how, thanks to the Islamic guidance of our god-fearing brothers and sisters, the heavenly rays of faith have penetrated their hearts. Upon leaving the prisons, these penitents will join in their multitudes to our faithful brothers and sisters, swelling the crowd of Muslims in our Islamic homeland. As far as their roles in *daraam* are concerned, these guilt-ridden individuals should always be portrayed as being mortified and ashamed for whatever treacheries they have committed in the past. Mind you, even in the *daraam* these penitents should not be left alone. They should be accompanied relentlessly by our eager revolutionary guards and Zainab Sisters so that they do not even dream for a moment of going astray from the path of righteous Muslims and joining the communists and anti-revolutionaries in those cursed safe houses. One of the great ayatollahs was …"

"Haaj Agha," I had to cut in, otherwise off he would go on again with his hocus-pocus, "with due respect, all of what you say is mentioned comprehensively in the licence and will be followed word for word."

"I have only come here as a humble messenger to give you some guidance," the minister whined. "Our expert brothers here present have also some comments to add." He turned to Ostaad Honarkhor and asked him to give his opinions about the art of drama.

"I have talked at length in my countless books," Ostaad Honarkhor stood up and began his speech, fidgeting, twitching his shoulders, and adjusting his glasses, "about my theories, as a good Muslim, on the art of writing short stories, novels of all genres, the techniques of composing poetry, the art of writing drama, the art of cinema, the art of photography, the ancient art of icon-painting, clay-work, carpet-weaving, Islamic architecture, and calligraphy. To put it in a nutshell, although the business of art emanates from an instinctive desire to create by following age-old techniques, this is not good art. Art is a powerful means of propaganda to serve only the divine ideals of the Islamic Republic. I humbly propose to you this serious question: by staging this play, do we have the intention of achieving these celestial goals?"

"That would not be Shakespeare's play," Othello could not help muttering gloomily. "It would be the mouthpiece of the reg …"

"Wait a sec, *babaa*," Iago said under his breath, nudging Othello hard in the ribs. "Let's see what comes out of this."

"But the core of the tragedy of *Othello* …" Othello persisted.

"We've talked at length about this subject." I had to remind him to be quiet. I turned to Ostaad Honarkhor and pleaded with him to go on.

"On that note," he said, "I humbly call upon Ostaad Safihollah to honour us by his inestimable erudition."

"In the Name of Allah the Merciful the Compassionate." Ostaad Safihollah stood up and began his speech in his self-possessed manner. "In the name of Allah who taught human beings to read and write. *Salaam* to the divine and innocent souls of all the messengers of Allah. *Salaam* to our revered Imam of our Islamic nation for whom we wish a very long life. *Salaam* also to our martyrs who have watered with their unblemished blood the gigantic tree of our beloved Islam. First, if I can be so bold as to recite a poem by a great Muslim scholar in order to shed some light on the principles of drama. This great philosopher-theologian says:

> *Christ breathed on to dead men,*
> *To bring them back to life.*
> *We take urine samples from the sick,*
> *To cure them from their mortal illnesses.*

33

"Taking urine samples from sick men in the past was one of the standard procedures practised by the alchemists and physicians," he carried on serenely, articulating each word. "Doctors these days in hospital labs examine the colour of our urine and the type of residues in it to determine what kind of diseases we suffer from." After a short pause he took up the thread of his learned discourse and said, "In another profound Islamic text on medicine and moral well-being, written by a renowned man of Allah, we come across a poem that says:

Oh, my sweetheart, I wish you were unwell,
And I wish I were sirop of opium and belladonna,
So that they could insert me up your arse.

"In the past," he went on to explain the significance of the poem, "they made a sirop of opium and belladonna and poured it into a dried-up goat's bladder. They then carefully inserted its nozzle into the back passage of the patient. This very popular medical procedure, called an enema, was known to be of great health benefits for patients who suffered from a variety of ailments. What I am getting at by reciting these mystical, albeit somewhat vulgar, poems and outdated medical procedures, is that it is our duty to go along with modern times and adapt the methods used commonly these days in our Islamic Republic. First and foremost, we should take urine samples from each of our artists to find out what sort of unholy diseases, both physical and moral, they're afflicted by."

Othello couldn't stop himself roaring with laughter, shaking his head.

"No, Jenab-e Othello." Ostaad Safihollah frowned at him. "You may find this rather amusing. It's evident that

34

you're not capable of understanding the symbolic and innovative aspect of this discourse. Our god-fearing doctors and medical technicians in the Ministry of Islamic Culture and Guidance test the urine samples of countless numbers of musicians, painters, actors, and entertainers from all segments of our society to make sure that our artists do not carry the noxious viruses of toppled monarchy, communism, the immoral Western civilisation, particularly the Great Satan of America and Zionism, to hatch plots against our fledgling Islamic Republic. If you think this is a sort of censorship carried out to nip in the bud the talents of our artists, well, I must inform you that you're wrong there."

He paused for a moment or two to gather his thoughts.

"Now we come to the topic of the insertion of the belladonna and opium sirop into the back passage of sick people about which the physicians of the times past have written copiously." He took up his medical exposition. "The insertion of this enema solution, by all accounts, worked very well against fever and constipation. This not only made the patient feel hale and hearty in his body but also made him feel morally elated and ecstatic. After this safe and rather enjoyable procedure is administered to our artists they will not only feel much better in their bodies, but also notice a marked improvement in their moral life. Only after undergoing this wonderful experience would they be able to serve wholeheartedly our young and unique Islamic Republic.

"You're more than welcome," he went on, "if you wish, to make a symbolic interpretation of all this. The insertion of opium and belladonna sirop, for instance, could be seen as the ideological guidance implanted inside you by our eminent ayatollahs to equip you in your struggles against the heathens and the Great Satan of America and its Zionist lackeys. The moral of all my preaching is that it is our Islamic duty to administer this procedure to our young drama artists."

Upon hearing this nonsense, Cassio and Iago, who were sitting on the edge of the platform, sprang to their feet as if stung by wasps. Othello sat calmly on his chair in brooding disbelief.

"What?" Iago said loudly, looking at me. "Are they going to take our stools?"

"I will not let them shove an opium sirop up my arse!" Cassio said.

"Oy, shut your gob and sit down," the revolutionary guard growled through his moustachioed mouth, pointing his Kalashnikov at them.

"My brother actors," the minister reassured them benignly, looking around the stage, "seeing, fortunately, that women are not among us, I can, with all honesty, reveal to you that we have not brought with us the necessary equipment to take your urine samples or insert opium sirop into any orifice in your bodies." He opened and spread out his *abaa*. "As you can see, nothing is concealed under my *abaa*."

"I have brought only a few of the books I've published in this briefcase." Ostaad Honarkhor opened his briefcase and displayed its contents.

"And there is nothing but official papers in my folders." Ostaad Safihollah followed suit by opening his folders and showing what was in them.

"I am grateful for the valuable counsel provided by the honourable experts." I addressed Sayyed Pashmeddin. "I wonder if, with your permission, we could now show you a sample of some of the scenes in the play."

"What did you say was the name of the play, brother director?" he asked.

"*Othello.*"

"*Baleh, baleh,* I know a thing or two about this *Atoghloo,*" he said, nodding. "He was, no doubt, a great master in his field, in the same class as the great French Islamologist Vaalter Escott. I have read in a book, written by a grand ayatollah on various subjects including the rituals of passing water or relieving yourself if you happen to be in the middle of a desert or a jungle or how to copulate with your wife in the middle of an earthquake, that St Oghugustus in his celebrated book on Christian Jurisprudence has sung the praises of this scholar as an eminent master in his own right. This distinguished Ostaad *Atoghloo* has written a book that I don't recall." He turned to Ostaad Safihollah and asked, "Ostaad, be kind enough to inform us about the title of this book."

"I believe it is called *The Art of How to be a Good Marionette.*" Ostaad Safihollah was pleased to show off his encyclopaedic knowledge. "In this book he discusses at length how we wretched human beings are nothing but helpless marionettes in the hands of that ultimate puppet-master – Allah the Merciful the Compassionate."

"Othello was not a writer," Othello sniggered, addressing the minister. "It's the name of a play written by Shakespeare."

"That's precisely what I said, brother," Sayyed Pashmeddin retorted with some heat. "This Ostaad *Shekespir* must have belonged to the people who followed a sacred book. Mustn't he?"

"He has written a lot of plays," Othello replied.

"No, no," Sayyed Pashmeddin said. "What I meant was that was he a believer of sacred scriptures and worshipped only one God."

"Yes, Haaj Agha." I had to intervene. "He was a god-fearing, practising Christian."

"He was not converted to our beloved Islam in his lifetime, then?" Sayyed Pashmeddin said, not seeming happy at all.

"Shakespeare lived long before our holy prophet, Haaj Agha." Ostaad Safihollah put his oar in.

"So he did," the minister said. "In that case, *Inshallah*, in the other world our holy prophet and twelve imams will intercede to Allah on his behalf to turn a blind eye to his sins when he was in this mean world. What was the name of this play?"

"*Othello*," I repeated.

"In my humble opinion," the minister said, "I suggest that you stage Ostaad *Sheksepir* in this play."

"Shakespeare is not the play." Cassio had to correct him.

"What is he then, brother?" the minister said, baffled.

"He was the playwright," Othello said.

"What difference does it make if you stage the playwright or the play?" the minister growled. "This is in direct opposition to slogan of our brave Muslim people who are on the stage at all hours of every day, demonstrating against the Great Satan."

"Haaj Agha," Ostaad Honarkhor, sensing the tense atmosphere, stepped in, "at the moment I'm in the process of writing a drama about this old master." He then went on in a pacifying tone, "Let's, with your kind consent, see what our brothers have to show us about this play."

"All right then," the minister agreed grudgingly. "So far I have not detected any problem. As a matter of personal interest only, I wonder if brother *Atoghloo*, as his Azeri name suggests, came from the Azerbaijan region."

"He was from Maghreb," Othello corrected him, "not Azerbaijan!"

"Oh, you mean the present day Morocco," the minister said, shaking his head. "Morocco is an Islamic country and has a cordial relationship with our Islamic Republic. In that case the divine lights of Allah had made the heart of brother *Sheksepir* glow with the light of Islam even before the coming of the Prophet Mohammad (the blessings of Allah be upon him and his clan). As regards his secret faith, he most certainly made it his mission to lead brother *Atoghloo* to the only path of righteousness that is the path of Islam. May Allah immerse him in His eternal mercy." He then turned to Ostaad Safihollah and said, "As you are a man of faith and a treasure-house of knowledge, maybe you can enlighten us more on this matter."

"Being one of the advisors in the Ministry of Islamic Guidance," Ostaad Safihollah began, more than pleased to air his views, "I approved the certificate for this play only because of the person of brother Othello, who was a renowned warlord, born and bred in our allied country, Morocco. This brother Othello loved wars and battles and could not live without them, just like our dear revolutionary guards who are nothing but instruments of war in the hands of Allah, just like their great ancestors in Saudi Arabia centuries ago. Othello strongly believed that war is a divine blessing and falls upon human beings like benedictions from heaven. War and bloodshed were always the main preoccupation of the Prophet and the men-of-Allah. The purpose of the nations they created was nothing but war after war. Everything served nothing but to sustain constant wars with other nations. All Othello dreamt about was battles or preparing himself for battlefields. He never took his armour off, always ready to be dispatched to wherever his masters commanded him to go. He did it because he believed in everlasting wars."

"So, without knowing it himself," Sayyed Pashmeddin pitched in, "he was one of the noble men who sowed the seeds of our beloved 'Army of Allah' that indeed appeared centuries later."

"That is undeniably true." Ostaad Honarkhor voiced his approval. "That is why I endorsed the staging of this drama. Do not lose sight of the fact that the black Muslims were always at war with other tribes and neighbouring countries."

"That's right," the minister hastened to remind his audience. "The *muezzin* of our beloved messenger of Allah was Bilal al-Habashi, who was an Ethiopian."

"Precisely so, Haaj Agha." I had to say something to please him. "That's the only reason we chose this drama. Othello's black colour plays a vital part in this drama."

"I couldn't agree more," Ostaad Honarkhor said. "Allow me to clarify some crucial points." He opened his briefcase, took out a book, found a page and said, "I have talked clearly about this matter in my book *Islamic Art*. On page 35 I have said that The Black Stone in holy Kaaba in Saudi Arabia is black because the colour of the large bulk of oppressed humanity throughout history was and is black. All the racist men in history believed that blackness is associated with evil. Even in our own folklore and literature black men were depicted as not only nasty, but stupid and clownish …"

"Where is this black Muslim brother, then?" the minister asked, looking round the stage.

"That man is our brother Othello, here." I pointed to Othello, who sprang to his feet.

"Is this him?" The minister eyed Othello up and down. "I have spent years studying four volumes called *Properties of Inanimate Objects, Animals, Plants, and Mankind* written by a great Islamic scholar. In the last volume on the Properties of Mankind he has written that the people of Morocco were black, therefore our brother *Atoghloo* must have been black. Why is it that our actor brother here is white?"

"Our make-up artist will make him look as black as charcoal," I rushed to explain.

"What do you mean by make-up?" the minister asked, vexed.

"We'll colour him black with special make-up charcoal."

"*Astaghforellah!*" the minister bellowed in Arabic. "You mean you're going to meddle with Allah's creation!"

"Not to worry, Haaj Agha." Ostaad Honarkhor was quick to cut in. "This special charcoal can easily be washed off with water."

"Praise be to Allah." Sayyed Pashmeddin heaved a sigh of relief, raising his hands heavenwards in the manner of a supplicant. Remembering something, he then added, "Hearing this, something important has crossed my mind. I wonder if the black hostages in the Nest of Spies (that is how the American Embassy was dubbed by the mollahs) are in fact white men who have daubed themselves with the so-called 'make-up' charcoal. We must remember to inform our brothers in the Nest of Spies to be on their guard."

"Not all of the black soldiers guarding the American Embassy were spies," Ostaad Honarkhor dared to advise. "As the poet fittingly says:

> *However hard you wash a man from Zanzibar,*
> *His skin will not become as white as snow.*

"Since we've taken them as hostages they have washed themselves several times and they are still black. All that soap and water would have washed off the charcoal off their bodies by now. As you know, they have remained as genuinely black as of the Black Stone in Kaaba. Those black hostages whom we released by the direct order of the Imam resemble our Moorish brother, Othello."

"*Laa elaaha ella Allah*," Sayyed Pashmeddin brayed in Arabic, slapping his knee. "The authorities responsible for the hostages are neglecting their Islamic duties. They should have herded these black hostages to a *hammam* and scrubbed them thoroughly to find out if they were genuinely black or, Allah forbid, white spies masquerading as latter-day *Atoghloos*.

Could you be kind enough to remind me later to bring up this matter of utmost national security in the next cabinet meeting?" he asked Ostaad Safihollah.

Ostaad Safihollah at once took out his notebook and scribbled some notes. A hush fell over everyone. Iago and Cassio stood statuelike in the middle of the stage. Othello, grim-faced, sat on the edge of the raised platform, contemplating his big toe. Sayyed Pashmeddin beaded his rosary, muttering some sort of curses in Arabic, as mollahs do when brooding over a grave matter.

"If you are ready," I addressed the minister, "with your permission, we can get on with the play."

"If the ostaads agree you may proceed," he said, casting glances to his right and left, "I'm all ears."

"Yes, yes," the two ostaads said loudly in unison, jiggling their heads like a pair of marionettes. "We are ready, too, Haaj Agha."

"Brother Cassio," I called out, "could you please nip backstage and ask our sisters to come in?"

Desdemona and Emilia, veiled from head to foot in black chadors, hurried back to the stage, followed by the Zainab Sister, and stood well away from the male actors. I asked Iago to go backstage and bring three glasses of tea for our guests. No sooner had he placed the tray of tea and sugar bowl on the table than Sayyed Pashmeddin and the ostaads grabbed the glasses, popped sugar lumps into their mouths, poured the tea into the saucers, and slurped their drinks noisily.

"Could you please tell us, as we talked about this before, who is the anti-revolutionary fellow in this *daraam*?" the minister asked, crunching the remaining sugar lump in his mouth.

"The one who brought you the tea tray." I pointed out Iago.

"Hands up!" The revolutionary guard pounced forward like a wild beast, pointing his Kalashnikov at Iago.

"May they wrap me in a shroud if I am anti-revolutionary," Iago said in a panic, putting his hands up. "I took part in all the anti-monarchy demonstrations."

"Is that all?" the revolutionary guard asked, stepping menacingly closer to Iago. "What did you actually do except walking in the streets and screaming against the tyranny of the monarchy?"

"I published some articles in a newspaper about how SAVAK tortured to death many of my student friends in the Evin Prison."

"Since when has writing articles become revolutionary action?" the revolutionary guard said. "I followed the advice of the Imam Khomeini and smashed the windows of sixty buildings. That's what I call revolutionary. I bet you didn't smash even a single one."

"I also smashed some windows." Iago was left with no choice but to resort to a lie to save his skin.

"Tell me how many, then, if you're man enough," the guard said, eager to see if Iago had done more damage than him.

"Sixty-one windows." Iago thought up a number worthy of a true revolutionary.

"Brother Iago is telling the truth." I had to back my friend up. "I was in the streets with him and I saw him in action with my own eyes; how enthusiastically he shattered those window glasses into shards with bricks and stones. I swear on the grave of my mother, I'm telling the truth."

"How many cinemas and cabarets did you set fire to?" the guard asked Iago to test further his commitment to the commands of the Imam.

"*Babaa*, I didn't have a chance to set fire to cinemas and cabarets," Iago insisted, getting more and more rattled and desperate for the brute to leave him alone.

"Gotcha!" the guard bawled triumphantly. "This proves that you're an anti-revolutionary."

"I swear to Allah and His Messenger," I cut in impatiently, "brother Iago is not anti-revolutionary."

"Didn't you say it yourself half an hour ago that he was an anti-revolutionary?"

"You got the wrong end of the stick, brother." I struggled to put him right. "Brother Iago is actually *acting* like an anti-revolutionary."

"If you act like someone," the guard spouted forth, "you will end up being like that person."

"You've a point there, brother guard," Ostaad Safihollah acknowledged, placing his glass in the saucer. "Only if you play the role of someone else at all times, no matter where you are and what you do." He then stood up, walked to the revolutionary guard, pulled him aside by his elbow and explained to him in confidence that all the necessary checks had been carried out on that Iago fellow and he was not an anti-revolutionary.

"Whatever you say, Ostaad," the guard said deferentially. He lowered his Kalashnikov and marched back to his post at the door.

"Haaj Agha," he said in a flattering voice, addressing Sayyed Pashmeddin, "we're only trying to do our duty ..."

"I perfectly understand, brother." The minister cut him short, motioning him to be quiet. He then turned to me and asked, pointing to Cassio, "I suppose this one plays the role of a penitent."

"Yes, Haaj Agha."

"Allah the Almighty has pardoned you with His infinite grace and has opened the doors of compassion to you," Sayyed Pashmeddin invoked solemnly, regarding Cassio with a mixture of pity and contempt. His face darkened and he asked him, "Have you been an anti-revolutionary in the past?"

"I was just an ordinary guy minding my own business," Cassio said respectfully. "In my spare time I was an amateur actor."

"What Haaj Agha means is that in your role in this drama, what system of beliefs do you hold on to?" Ostaad Honarkhor said.

"All I know is that I play the role of Cassio. Maybe you tell them about my beliefs," he asked me.

"That means, what were your beliefs before you played the role of Cassio who is a repentant in the play?" Ostaad Honarkhor could not keep quiet.

"At the start of the play Iago has described Cassio's character very well," I said and addressed Iago. "Brother Iago, could you please recite the relevant piece from the script?"

Iago frantically flipped through the script and began to read from the middle of a dialogue:

"*But he …*" he began to recite in a dramatic tone.

"Iago is referring to this brother who stands here," I explained, nudging Cassio forward.

"*But he, as loving his own pride and purposes, / Evades them with a bombast circumstance/ Horribly stuffed with epithets of war, / Nonsuits my mediators,*" Iago went on.

"What kind of a penitent is this man, brother director?" the minister asked.

"This is an anti-revolutionary fellow who is talking about him, Haaj Agha," I rushed to clarify. "If you'll be kind enough to wait, you'll hear more."

I told Iago to skip two verses and read on:

"*Forsooth, a great arithmetician,*
One Michael Cassio, a Florentine –"

At this point, Iago mumbled, skipping over six compromising verses about Cassio being damned and mocked at for having a fair wife and the fact that he most likely was to become a cuckolded husband. These verses would not go down well with the officials. He found the most relevant verses that described Cassio in the middle of the dialogue and proudly recited them:

"... *Mere prattle without practice*
Is all his soldiership."

"Did you hear that, Haaj Agha?" Cassio was quick to redeem himself. "Now you can see that I'm not an anti-Islamic activist."

"You're absolutely right, brother Cassio," Sayyed Pashmeddin agreed gleefully. "Listening to these verses proves beyond a shadow of a doubt that you're a genuine penitent. You must now completely forget about your past sins and never give in to the temptations of Satan, neither the one who was kicked out of paradise by Allah nor the Great Satan of America here in this mean world." He then said to me, "Now you can tell me all about the roles of those two sisters in the play, brother director."

"That sister on the left plays the role of Desdemona," I pointed at her, "who's the wife of Othello."

"Is this sister married to brother *Atoghloo* according to Sharia Law?" Sayyed Pashmeddin asked, stroking his beard and eyeing Desdemona with a mixture of piety and the lustfulness of an old-time mollah.

"Yes, Haaj Agha," I confirmed. "They were married with an impeccable Islamic marriage contract in the presence of a fully-qualified mollah."

"I personally congratulate them for undertaking such an auspicious Islamic obligation," drawled Sayyed Pashmeddin. "May both of them live as virtuous husband and wife for ever."

"How about the other sister over there?" Sayyed Pashmeddin nodded towards Emilia. "Is she also married?"

"She's the lawful wife of brother Iago." I made it crystal clear.

"What was the name of that brother?" Sayyed Pashmeddin pointed to Cassio.

"His name is Cassio."

"Is this brother married?"

"He's got a mistress," I blurted out and immediately clapped my hand over my mouth,–realising that I'd made the most foolish blunder. "Her name is Bianca. Unfortunately, she was not able to come today due to other commitments."

"Mistress!" Sayyed Pashmeddin echoed loudly, jumping up in sudden anger from his chair.

"It's obvious why she's not here today," the Zainab Sister jeered, having hitherto sat in silence.

"Not to worry, sister," barked the guard. "The *Monkaraat* Unit will sort her out."

"*Jenaab-e Hojjat-ol-eslam*." I had to explain away my gaffe. "This is a play written long ago by an English dramatist."

"Whether English or not English, written at present or in the past, you know very well that to have a kept woman in an Islamic country is against Sharia Law," Sayyed Pashmeddin fumed, spluttering through his hennaed beard. "As a matter of fact, this is the same as propagating prostitution." He then turned to the two officials and said, "Brothers, make sure to inform the *Monkaraat* Unit about this as soon as we're back in the Ministry. My brothers in the Ministry of Culture and Islamic Guidance are inundated with mountains of work and are not able to deal, single-handedly, with any other moral corruption in the country."

"A quick phone call will do the job." The guard was quick to offer his help.

"Where, brother?" Sayyed Pashmeddin asked.

"To Haaj Agha Ghassaal to send some guards over."

"To do what?"

"To take this adulterous son of a gun to the *Monkaraat*."

On hearing this, we all regarded each other in alarm. I quickly thought I'd better beg Ostaad Honarkhor to intercede.

"Ostaad, could you *please* try to explain to our brother guard here that this is a *play*!"

He stood up, walked to the guard and calmly explained to him that the actors were only acting and everything, if he would have a bit of patience, would eventually be Islamic at the end.

Fed up with all this badgering by these half-wits, Cassio grabbed hold of my elbow and pulled me aside.

"As far as I'm concerned, Behrouz," he whispered in my ear, "I'm done with this production. I'm serious. Minutes ago they impeached me for being one of those penitents, now they accuse me of being adulterous. Next, they will take me to the *Monkaraat* and only the devil knows what'll happen to me and where will I end up after that."

Distraught, he pleaded with Sayyed Pashmeddin. "Haaj Agha, I'm a married man with two kids. I lead an ordinary, decent life,"

"Why, then, have you taken a mistress?"

"Who said I've got a fancy woman?" Cassio said. "All this happens in the play."

"If you allow me, Haaj Agha," I intervened, "we thought about changing this bit. As the presence of a

49

mistress in this drama goes against Sharia Law, we will completely remove that bit. In fact, brother Cassio's lawfully-married wife is now going to play the role of Bianca."

"Since when did my wife become an actress, may I ask?" Cassio muttered, looking at me crossly. "She's just a housewife, for God's sake."

"From now on she'll play the role of your lawful wife in the play!" I said, winking at him to keep quiet. "You get my drift, don't you?" I whispered.

At that moment the door of the hall was opened and Bianca rushed in. She started to take off her scarf, but, seeing the minister and the officials, she quickly put it back in place. She climbed up to the stage and looked at everyone as if she had seen some ghosts.

"I apologise for …" she mumbled.

"And who would this sister be?" Sayyed Pashmeddin asked me, interrupting her.

"B … B … Bianca."

"You think we're donkeys and don't understand anything." The Zainab Sister gave a screech like a hellcat from under the hem of her chador, glaring at Bianca. "As a revolutionary Muslim woman I understand very well the meaning of her name. I know for sure that her real name is in fact *Binekaah*, meaning an unmarried woman who sleeps around with anyone who takes her fancy, as a whore does! I know all about sluts like you, as I was …"

"I think you've made your point." The minister had to tighten her leash again, before she revealed too much of where she really had sprung from.

"That's what a mistress really is, Haaj Agha," Zainab Sister snarled, not giving a fig about his warning.

"My sister's right, Haaj Agha." The revolutionary guard backed her up. "That's what they call her."

Ignoring everyone, the Zainab Sister walked to Bianca and violently pulled her scarf down to her eyebrows.

"The way things are going," Othello, grim-faced, said to me, "I think it's about time we kissed goodbye to this production. We already have enough farce going on here."

"Not at all, brother *Atoghloo*," Sayyed Pashmeddin said, overhearing him. "As Ostaad Honarkhor rightly made it perfectly clear, we need the art of *daraam* that is of pivotal importance to us, in the same way that the ancient religious entertainment of *ta'zieh* served and carries on serving our Shiite ideals to keep our creed alive. As long as everything complies with Sharia Law, all will be fine and legitimate."

"But nothing is committed against Sharia Law here, Haaj Agha," I politely informed him.

"Not to worry at all, brother director," Sayyed Pashmeddin said. "Allah the Merciful the Compassionate has, in His infinite wisdom, provided us with keys for every calamity and knotty problems in our short sojourn here in this base world. Our beloved Prophet is known to have also said to his disciples that with every disease, Allah has sent us an accompanying cure and all we have to do is to search for them. So, to make this dilemma of the mistress disappear like magic, I will, this very minute, make sister *Binekaah* the temporary wife of brother *Kaassyho* by making her his *siegheh*."

He then began to declaim in Arabic the *siegheh* formula. Once he was done, he leaned forward and took a sugar lump from the sugar bowl and handed it to Cassio to sweeten his mouth. He took another sugar lump and gave it to Bianca.

"You can now sweeten your mouths to mark this hallowed occasion of matrimony," Sayyed Pashmeddin said solemnly. "May you live together in happy wedlock, albeit a short while, *inshallah*."

Cassio and Bianca contemplated one another in silence for a moment. Cassio, for fear of more accusations, nibbled a little at the sugar lump.

"I just came to let you know that I can't take part in this play," Bianca said. "I'm very sorry."

She then chucked the sugar lump on the floor and made for the door.

"I know very well that you're off to get on with your real profession," the Zainab Sister shrieked after her, spitting on the floor to show her disgust. "Haa, she thinks that she can fool us. You can creep into any hole you like to do your sinful job in this city. Only remember that, sooner or later, you'll be ferreted out like a dirty rat by our brothers and sisters."

The Zainab Sister realised that she was talking to herself like a madwoman, because Bianca had long ago left the hall.

"Shame on you." The revolutionary guard, thinking himself a good Muslim, decided to rebuke Cassio. "How could you just stand there and do nothing about the honour of your lawfully-married wife?"

An uncomfortable silence fell over the stage. For fear of being accused of more bizarre sins against Sharia Law, the actors stood mute and motionless, gazing into space.

"I wonder if we could get on with our rehearsal, Haaj Agha." Our show must go on, and it was getting late.

"I see no objection, now." Sayyed Pashmeddin gave his consent. "As you have managed to eliminate that rotten apple, that *Binekaah* woman, from amongst your decent

52

brothers and sisters who have proved so far to be good Muslims."

"Now that all my actor brothers and sisters are all cleared from all possible sins against Islam, we can go on rehearsing Act 2 Scene 3 from the play. In this scene the action takes place in Othello's castle."

"No, no, no, brother director." Sayyed Pashmeddin stopped me there. "You must no longer use the word 'castle'. That is a reminder of the times of tyranny of the Pahlavis' regime. If you recall the sermons of Imam Khomeini in his first speech upon returning from exile, he justly said that castle-dwellers, after being vanquished, had all fled the country and that hovel-dwellers were now ruling the land. So the word 'hovel' is more appropriate than 'castle'. May I remind you also that our glorious Muslim commanders in the past lived, not in grand castles, but in humble dwellings akin to hovels. So bear this in mind when you decide upon the final design for what you call scenery in your profession."

"You're absolutely right." I agreed at once. "I'll bear that in mind. Now then, let's imagine that the action is taking place in Othello's hovel. It's a wretched little room in a mudbrick house. Its floor is covered with a tattered kilim. In one corner stands a paraffin-stove and in the far corner all the mattresses, bed linen and pillows are piled up. A wooden trunk for clothes stands in one corner. Brother Othello, sister Desdemona, and sister Emilia are standing in the room." I then asked the actors to begin.

The actors cleared their throats and assumed their poses. When ready, Othello turned to Cassio and said in a dramatic voice:

Good Michael, look you to the guard tonight:
Let's teach ourselves that honourable stop
Not to outsport discretion.

"*Iago hath direction what to do/But notwithstanding, with my personal eye/Will I look to't,*" Cassio said.

"*Iago is most honest/Michael, goodnight: tomorrow with your earliest/Let me have speech with you/Goodnight.*" Othello turned to Desdemona. "*Come, my dear love …*"

"My dear what?" Sayyed Pashmeddin interrupted. "Aren't these two a lawfully-married couple?"

"Yes, they are, Haaj Agha, as I mentioned before."

"We Muslims never call our wives 'my dear love'," Sayyed Pashmeddin said heatedly. "What's all this nonsense about?"

"What are we supposed to call them then?" Othello asked.

"The corrupt westernised people talk like that," Sayyed Pashmeddin replied. "We call our wives, depending on who and what we are, such terms as better half, woman of the house, the one indoors, missis, the weaker one."

"But none of these are mentioned in the text." Othello dared to contradict him.

"Let's forget about what it says in the text," Sayyed Pashmeddin retorted, "and stick to words and phrases that won't inflame sexual desire and lust in our Muslim compatriots.

"*Come, my woman of the house!*" Othello bellowed in a manly voice, "*The purchase made, the fruits are to ensue …*"

"From what I hear it appears that this brother *Atoghloo* was not only one of the bravest generals of his time," Sayyed Pashmeddin was pleased to find out, "but also belonged to the respectful community of merchants in the bazaar of his city."

"With respect, Haaj Agha," I had to clarify Shakespeare's use of a figure of speech to stop the minister from even more amusing misunderstandings, "Othello had nothing to do with the merchants in the bazaar of his city. Shakespeare here is making use of metaphor to tell us that Othello's marriage is not yet consummated because of his too many engagements in the battlefields."

"In that case, in my humble opinion, brother *Atoghloo* should've consummated his marriage before he went off to fight the enemy," Sayyed Pashmeddin argued. "Our beloved Prophet and the commanders at the glorious dawn of Islam never went to their never-ending battles before they consummated their marriages. That comes before any other Islamic duty."

"You're right once again," I said, now truly at the end of my rope, "but Othello was in a mortal hurry to be dispatched to another war at any minute."

"If you say so, brother director," Sayyed Pashmeddin conceded grudgingly.

"All right then, let's crack on with the rehearsal," I said. "Now, brother Othello and sister Desdemona exit, leaving brother Cassio on his own on the stage. Brother Iago then enters the stage. Please, you may go on, brothers."

"*Welcome, Iago: we must to the watch,*" Cassio said.

"*Not this hour, lieutenant ...*" Iago replied.

"Lieutenant?" Ostaad Safihollah objected. "In the Islamic Republic, established by and for the dispossessed of this world, we're all equal before Allah. Therefore everybody should call one another brother. The title 'lieutenant' implies hierarchy; that's not permissible in our beloved religion."

"Not this hour, lieutenant brother ..." Iago corrected himself.

"I made it clear that brother is enough," Ostaad Safihollah insisted.

"Not this hour, brother: 'tis not yet ten o'th'clock. Our general cast us thus early for the love of his Desdemona, who let us not therefore blame: he hath not yet made wanton the night with her, and she is sport for Jove," Iago finally said.

"She's a most exquisite lady," Cassio said.

"And, I'll warrant her, full of game," Iago said.

"Indeed, she's a most fresh and delicate creature," Cassio agreed.

"It looks as if we're witnessing a place in which corruption, adultery and prostitution are rampant!" Sayyed Pashmeddin remarked, addressing the two ostaads, who also looked outraged.

"I am wholeheartedly of the same opinion as Hojjat-ol-eslam Pashmeddin," Ostaad Honarkhor declared, standing up. "I must say a few things of grave moment: brother Iago said that brother Othello and sister Desdemona have not yet slept together and have not consummated their marriage." He then regarded Iago with accusing eyes and said, "You talk as if you were hiding in the married couple's bedroom to make sure that they did it. Tell me if I'm wrong."

"I swear on the grave of my mother, I have never been into anybody's bedroom in my whole life," Iago pleaded.

"Can you tell me where did you hear about such intimate goings-on that can only happen between a man and his wife in the privacy of their bedroom?" Ostaad Honarkhor persisted.

"I think Shakespeare is the one who should take the blame, not my friend here." Othello decided to come to Iago's rescue. "You see, the dramatist is cunningly putting these words into Iago's mouth so that he can awaken in Cassio's mind some lustful feelings towards Desdemona."

"If that's the case, brother Othello," Ostaad Honarkhor said, pleased to find Othello's interpretation as a perfect back-up for whatever obscene ideas he had already grasped so far, "this brother Iago has not only been propagating prostitution, he also has the respectable profession of procuring ladies for those rich lackeys in the overthrown Pahlavi regime."

"I don't have the faintest clue what you're talking about," Iago said, frustrated. "I gave up my teaching job a year ago. In order to support my family, I've been carting passengers around Tehran in my rented cab. All my life I liked theatre and acting. Whenever I got a chance I used to go and see all sorts of plays in theatres in and around Lalezaar. Drama being my passion, some evenings I do some acting without expecting any rewards whatsoever. These absurd accusations about me are nothing but fantasies of …"

"Ostaad Honarkhor is surely referring to the character of Iago in the play, not your real person in everyday life." I had to stop Iago before he brought even more trouble upon himself.

"You told me yourself I'm Iago, aren't I?"

"*Baba*, you're acting as Iago in the play, aren't you?" I told Iago and looked around at everyone. "We also know who you are outside this blasted play, don't we? Iago of the play is an evil son of a bitch, right?"

"Hmm, this is becoming more and more exciting." The revolutionary guard sniggered. "Now it's come to light that this guy is a bastard, too."

"Brother guard," the minister said, "let's see what will come out of all this." He instructed Iago to go on with the rehearsal.

As the next six lines were all about how pretty Desdemona was, with some raunchy descriptions of her body and a reference to the nuptial bed, Iago by now knew that reciting these lines would provide them with more excuses to drag him even deeper into the cesspool of their archaic punishment system. So he thought it best to skip them, as self-censorship was now becoming part of the whole farcical drama of staging a great Western tragedy in a country infested by Sharia Law.

"Come, brother, I have a stoup of wine, and here without are a brace of Cyprus gallants that ..." Iago recited.

"Bah! A jug of wine?" the revolutionary guard bawled, jumping on to the middle of the stage. "Out with it. Where have you hidden it?"

"Hang on a sec, brother," I intervened. "Brother Iago said that outside a couple of young men from Cyprus ..."

"All I know is that you've hidden a jug of wine somewhere," the guard yelled, almost poking his Kalashnikov into my ribs. "Come on, where is it?"

"I swear there's no such thing as a jug of wine anywhere here," I pleaded. "Once the actors leave the stage they'll drink wine that is supposed to be outside the stage and the audience will not see it. All this is going on within the drama."

"I don't care if they drink wine outside the *Caafeh* Daraam, *Caafeh* Karaamat or *Caafeh* Crystaal," the guard said. He then planted himself in front of Othello and ordered him to open his mouth and breathe out.

"Haaaa." Othello breathed out noisily at close range to the guard's face.

"You don't have to open your mouth that wide like a donkey in heat," the guard said, grimacing.

"This is the way I've always haaaed," Othello said, not taking his eyes off the guard.

The guard walked up to Cassio and ordered him to breathe out.

"Haaaaaaaaaa …"

"All right, all right." The guard drew back. "That's enough."

The guard started to walk up to Iago, looking more ominous.

"You've definitely drunk some *arrack*," the guard told him. "It's impossible that an anti-revolutionary communist like you wouldn't drink *arrack*."

Reluctant to breathe out, Iago stepped a few paces back and stood motionless, not for a moment taking his eyes off the guard.

I could not just stand there and watch this malarkey go on.

"Jenaab-e Minister," I said, "these brothers and sisters are not the types who drink and commit deeds prohibited by Sharia Law."

"Brother director," the minister moaned, "I do not have the authority to prevent my brother guard from doing his revolutionary duties. I would myself be in serious trouble if I tried to stop him. I take your word for it that they have not drunk any alcoholic beverages. To be on the side of caution, however, it would be best for all concerned if my brothers and sisters did a bit of harmless haaaaing."

Upon hearing this, the guard began to move closer to Iago who, in turn, started to walk backwards.

"If you think you can escape from this, you're wrong," the guard told him, pointing his Kalashnikov at him. "Go on, open your mouth wide and make a hearty 'haaa' like a man."

"Stop shilly-shallying and make a 'haaa', brother Iago," I urged him.

Finally, Iago decided to put an end to this and made a feeble quick 'haaa' to the guard's face.

"Although I don't like that guy in a robe, he definitely knows how to make a good mannish 'haaa'," the guard declared and walked back to the door. He then asked the Zainab Sister to do the same with the actresses. First, she walked up to Desdemona.

"Cover your face and open your mouth," she squawked at her, sticking her face into Desdemona's.

Desdemona made a quick 'haaa'.

"Pooh, pooh," the Zainab Sister said, fanning her face with the hem of her chador, "these women stink of perfume."

She then planted herself in front of Emilia and asked her to open her mouth and do the same. Emilia made an even quicker 'haaa', staring at her like a mischievous little girl.

"They haven't drunk anything so far," Zainab Sister said, evidently disappointed, and walked back to her sentry post before the door.

Everybody remained as quiet and still as mannequins in a tailor's workshop except Othello, who mumbled and gesticulated heatedly as if trying to convince an invisible person incapable of understanding his side of the argument.

"I've had enough of all this, I really have," he said more loudly. "To hell with *Othello*, Shakespeare, theatre, play-acting and this ludicrous … puppet show. Come to think of it, the way this rehearsal is going we'll all end up doing a *ta'zieh* in some square or other, all dressed up in Arabic garb! I think I've done and seen enough drama for today. I've made up my mind. I've decided to pack it in."

"Shut your gob and sit down," the guard and the Zainab Sister barked at him like two rabid dogs.

Seeing my friend Othello in that state, it dawned on me that there was a finality in his shaking voice. I myself had had enough of this tiresome buffoonery which had surpassed the boundaries of absurd behaviour that can be committed by human beings. I looked around at my friends. The men in their makeshift Shakespearean get-ups and women in their Islamic hijabs looked like a bunch of children draped in clumsily-made costumes about to perform a play in school which had been called off. I could read the same air of despair and desolation in their faces. One by one they glanced mutely at me as if trying to tell me something that I had already worked out. I decided to speak out for all of us.

"*Jenaab-e Hojjat-ol-eslam*," I addressed the minister calmly, "can I please beg of you to exempt us from staging this drama by withdrawing our licence."

"No way, Agha Director," the minister replied at once as if he sensed, ravenlike, what was coming. "On the contrary, you must go on with the rehearsal until you finish the job in hand. As the proverb says: better never to begin than never to make an end. That's why we've taken the trouble of coming here – to see your play. Only by attending dens of so-called cultural activities such as this will we be able to root out the weeds of corruption. Do not lose sight of the fact that a committee of faithful and upright men from the *Monkaraat* Unit and the Ministry of Islamic Culture and Guidance is formed to watch diligently over supposed cultural activities. I, for one, am satisfied with the conscientious efforts these dedicated brothers have put into this arduous Islamic duty. They do all this out of the goodness of their hearts to serve our Islamic Republic, asking for no rewards whatsoever but a modicum of thankfulness and prayers from the ordinary folk and the Imam himself who has nothing to say to them but praise. On that note I will beg of Ostaad Safihoddin here to add his valued observations on this matter."

Ostaad Safihoddin stood up, sorted out his jacket with his elbows, coughed a little and said, "I think, if I may, my brother Ostaad Honarkhor is more qualified than me to give his expert opinion on these subjects. Please, Ostaad."

Ostaad Honarkhor, ready as always to air his views on almost anything to do with culture, sprang to his feet.

"I'm of the opinion that this scene of wine-drinking by a gang of louts must be completely deleted," he asserted in the manner of a big-headed, all-knowing drama critic, "for the obvious reason that from the point of view of drama writing it is devoid of divine aesthetics and sublime human values."

"Just like that," Othello said. "Every minute we hear some unheard-of original ideas today. No one has ever dared to even think of doing such a thing."

"Well, brother Othello," Ostaad Honarkhor held forth, "if something doesn't fit into our Islamic world-view, we tear it into pieces, put it back together the way we want it to be, and then incorporate it into our own ideological outlook. In a nutshell, we transmute, through the alchemy of Islamic ideology, Western art and cultural products so that they will have an Islamic essence and appearance. I do not need to remind you of Imam Khomeini's speech to a bunch of writers and intellectuals in which he told them to write about nothing but Islam, otherwise good Muslims have a holy duty to snatch their pens and smash them into pieces. "

All this claptrap put me in mind of Dr Frankenstein who, in his enthusiasm to create a human being, made several trips to a charnel house, chopped off different body parts of dead and decaying mortals, and carted them to his laboratory. Once there, he sewed the organs together in the right place. After sticking electric wires into the stitched-up body, he passed electric currents into it. Instead of creating a human being, he created the most terrifying creature that was neither a human nor a monster. I wondered what sort of art this Islamic abomination would look like in that gruesome future that was awaiting us in my homeland.

"In that case," Othello said, "we should right now kiss goodbye to this production and chuck it in the bin." He then added after a short pause, "Will you do the same thing with our great poets and writers, I wonder?"

"If it deemed necessary, yes," Ostaad Honarkhor replied without a moment's hesitation.

Othello's expression darkened, as if he were gazing into something terrifying of which I was becoming more and more conscious. This was the future in which even our poets and writers would become the innocent victims whose works would be mutilated under the repeated assaults made by the bludgeon-brandishing of the barbaric, bearded Muslim thugs in turbans.

Hearing Othello's remarks, Ostaad Safihoddin stood up again and addressed him.

"Brother Othello, we have no intention of stopping you from staging this play or interfering in any way with the works of art created by our masters in the past. All we have in mind is to make sure this drama complies with the new culture begotten by our Islamic revolution. We do not have any ulterior motive, none whatsoever."

He then turned to the minister, who was tugging at his beard and muttering to himself.

"Haaj Agha, I beseech you not to lose your temper for the time being. All the obscene and immoral scenes in the play will be dealt with by our highly-qualified mollahs in the Ministry of Islamic Culture and Guidance, who know how to transform a text infested with depravity into a pure and uplifting Islamic one, *inshallah*." He drew a noisy breath. "If I can be bold enough, with your permission, to suggest a simple solution out of this impasse we are in, it would be a good idea if we see the rehearsal of the end of the play that, in my humble opinion, is acted in accordance with the Islamic criteria set out by Sharia Law that respects the honour of an insulted decent man who is none other than our brother Othello here. What is your opinion, Jenaab-e Minister?"

"I've no objection," the Minister said. "As a matter of fact, our holy Prophet has said in a sacred *hadith* that it would be of more benefit to start a *daraam* from the end and work back to the beginning of it. In this way we will know, right from the word go, what kind of a *daraam* is going to unfold in front of our eyes so that we can make up our minds whether to sit and watch it or walk out and go about our more important daily affairs. Our honest Muslim folks have even a nice little proverb that goes something like this: "Don't count your chickens before … what?"

"… they're hatched," Othello finished the sentence and added with heavy sarcasm, "Only then would one be able to eat them."

Sayyed Pashmeddin found Othello's remark rather amusing and, chuckling loudly through his beard, pushed his turban a little back on his head. Seeing him chortle, the two ostaads began a smothered laughter with their shoulders bobbing up and down. The revolutionary guard joined in the merriment and burst into loud guffaws. Abandoning her fake prudishness, the Zainab Sister also appreciated Othello's witticism and laughed along with the rest.

"Contrary to popular belief, we men of Allah enjoy, from time to time, witty remarks aimed at us," Sayyed Pashmeddin said, pushing his turban forward to its proper place on his head. "It's good to see that our unsmiling brother Othello can show a bit of a sense of humour."

He then cast a hard look at the guard and the Zainab Sister, who were still tittering like a pair of fools. They at once stopped, putting on their usual sour expressions.

Ostaad Honarkhor stood up, fidgeted and adjusted his glasses. "I must let you know that in my numerous books I have held Shakespeare in highest possible esteem. Right now I am in the process of writing a book in which I am endeavouring to prove by consulting authentic documents that Shakespeare was, in reality, a half-caste Iranian who lived in the south of Iran near the Persian Gulf. His father was an Arab Sheikh who married a young Iranian woman. They had several children, the youngest of whom was called Zubayr, who was destined to become Shakespeare, as we know him. Zubayr grew up with both Iranians and Arabs, becoming fluent in both languages.

"When young he earned his bread by cultivating palm trees, the fruits of which he sold in the local market to both Arabs and Iranians. Being incurably romantic, he fell in love with a daughter of an influential Iranian Sheikh who was the mortal enemy of Zubayr's father. Upon hearing Zubayr's secret passion, he just laughed, thinking that his son had lost his marbles. He ordered his son not to mention the name of the young beauty, never, ever again. Heart-broken, Zubayr found consolation in reading and composing love ditties and *ghazals* for his sweetheart during his solitary strolls along the Shatt-al-Arab River. Having a good knowledge of Arabic due to his commerce with Arab traders across the Gulf, he soon began to recite the Koran in his beautiful bass voice to his companions. Some hot summer evenings as they gathered under the palm trees, he sang some of his poems accompanied by the melancholy sound of a flute.

"As Shiite Islam was taking root in Iran, thanks to the heroic efforts of Shah Abbas the Great, religious plays in the form of *ta'zieh* were becoming popular all over the Safavid Empire. One day a mollah, a fervent advocate of Shiism, overheard, by chance, Zubayr's beautiful voice and asked him if he could sing and act in a *ta'zieh* during the upcoming month of Moharram. Flattered by this, young Zubayr took up the offer and performed his first ever role as an actor. His talent flourished and in no time he became a celebrity in the province.

"When his father passed away, Zubayr, still young, came to be known as Sheikh Zubayr. All his sisters soon married Arab traders, leaving him with his old mother, who very soon followed her husband to a better world. Lonely and heartbroken, he decided to say goodbye to his relatives and friends and cross the Gulf in a fisherman's dingy to go to Saudi Arabia and live in the vicinity of Kaaba, and devote his life to Allah. Through reading the Koran his fertile imagination was fired by the ancient stories retold in in the sacred book. Upon hearing the work of the great Arab poets during poetry recitals, he memorised them and soon began to compose some poems in Arabic himself. In no time he was turned into a kind of poet laureate, respected by the poetry-loving Bedouin Arabs. He came to learn about different cultures from the Muslims who flocked into the holy city of Mecca from all over the Islamic Empire. In this way he gathered a huge repertoire of stories from nearly everywhere. In his lonely hours, however, he composed *ghazals* for his sweetheart, whom he never forgot.

"One day a British spy, disguised as an adventure-seeking traveller, who was fluent in Arabic, spotted Sheikh Zubayr at a poetry festival and was hugely impressed by his poems. After the show he approached Zubayr and struck up a conversation with him. Zubayr was fascinated by the traveller's tales of exotic foreign lands and asked if he could accompany him on his travels. The astute traveller agreed at once, knowing that he could make someone great of this young Irano-Arab poet. In every inn, caravanserai, or village square Zubayr recited poetry and acted to earn his living.

"After visiting famous cities such as Cairo, Baghdad, Istanbul, and Venice, the two men finally boarded a merchant ship to England. By this time Zubayr had already picked up a considerable English vocabulary, phrases and sentences from his guiding companion who was keen to teach him that language, for he had his own secret designs for the young man.

"Once arrived at a small town in England, the townsfolk stared at Sheikh Zubayr, curious. They found his attire and his deep guttural accent quite charming. The longer he stayed, the more he enjoyed the company of the English people. He took great pleasure in expressing himself freely as no one was telling him how to think. When, for the first time, on the advice of his friend, he watched a play performed in the town's square by a travelling theatre troupe, he laughed heartily as he found it rather funny and very unlike the *ta'ziehs* in Iran. He immediately took a special interest in this kind of performing art. He watched many of these plays and at the same time improved his English by reading all sorts of poetic, dramatic and historical texts. One day the traveller suggested to him that Zubayr could translate and perform in the town's square one of the romantic Arabic poems he knew so well. Keen to show his God-given gift, Zubayr jumped at the offer and performed the popular tragic *Raheem and Raaheleh* narrative poem that he later developed into the drama, *Romeo and Juliet*.

The audience enjoyed the lyrics and the acting of this handsome foreign man with his swarthy complexion. Upon a nudge of encouragement from his protector adapted a *ta'zieh*, turning the martyred Imam Hossein into a tragic hero who dies so that justice would prevail. Some out-of-work actors were more than happy to try their acting skills in this new version of *ta'zieh*. They all learnt their parts. Some men wore burnous and Arabic headdresses, and others covered themselves in black veils, pretending to be the Arab women who accompanied the Prince of the Martyrs to the battlefield of Karbala. Many of the English men and women in the motley audience found this Arabic tragedy very sad indeed and wept helplessly.

"Heartened by this success, Zubayr began to adapt some of the classic Persian and Arab stories into English drama. By now he had many friends who were always ready to take part in his plays. As time passed he came to be known among the townsfolk as Shakespeare, as they found the name Sheikh Zubayr a bit of a tongue-twister.

"The traveller, being very well aware of Queen Elizabeth's passion for first-class entertainment, decided to contact the court officials, telling them about the fledgling dramatist in town. Queen Elizabeth, who had cordial dealings with the Muslim Ottoman Empire of the time and countries such as Morocco, agreed, out of curiosity, to watch one of the tragedies written and performed by this newcomer named Shakespeare. Being a shrewd monarch, she realised that she had stumbled upon a genius who could be a great asset to the art and literature of her reign, ensuring that she would be remembered for all time as the patron of good-quality drama. After watching so many of Shakespeare's plays – comedies, farces, historical tragedies, pastoral-comical, historical-pastoral, tragical-historical, tragical-comical-historical-pastoral, tragic *ta'ziehs* – she decided to make him the official bard of her court. As to the traveller, he formed a theatre company and made a fortune out of Shakespeare's plays. But Shakespeare never abandoned his true faith and remained a true follower of Islam, albeit secretly. Once a Muslim, always a Muslim, as they say. "

I sat there gobsmacked at hearing such a string of mumbo-jumbo put together so convincingly as to fool anyone who did not know a smattering of English history.

"A well-told true story, Ostaad." Sayyed Pashmeddin praised him, though he was yawning. "I am certain this was precisely what happened. Our brother *Shekespir* was none other than our pious Muslim Sheikh Zubayr who was treacherously enticed by a secret agent, disguised as a traveller, sent off on a mission to Saudi Arabia by British Imperialists. Praise be to Allah that brother *Shekespir* adhered to our beloved Islam till he died. May Allah bless his soul as all these great men were divine beings, sent down to us sinners by Allah to guide us on the path to eternal salvation. They were all, in reality, Muslims without being aware of it. As our great scholar Dr Elaahi Shamoortinejaad, who is the depository of all knowledge, enlightens us that all great men and women are born Muslims without knowing it."

"Now that you've proved without a shadow of a doubt that Shakespeare was really an Irano-Arab Muslim," Othello said, "please give us your final verdict on the drama of Othello."

"In my future book, dedicated entirely to the study of the tragedy of *Othello*," Ostaad Honarkhor said, quick to expound on another attribute of his all-embracing theory concerning the art of drama, "I have made it absolutely clear that the recasting and remoulding of the text of this drama must be inspired by our understanding of the divine aesthetic. This is because this drama is all about defending the chastity of the family and, above all, safeguarding the honour of our wives that is the obligation of all honest Muslim men."

"If that's the case," Othello said, shifting from foot to foot, "I wonder if you could guide us through the rest of the rehearsals."

As Ostaad Honarkhor evidently did not have the faintest clue as how to apply his cloud-cuckoo-land notions to the practicalities of such a complex drama, Ostaad Safihollah thought it his duty to come to the rescue with a brilliant solution to take us out of this impasse for which only good old Shakespeare was to blame.

"Forgive me, Brother Othello," Ostaad Safihollah said after standing up, "without being disrespectful to our divine poet Hafez, who memorised the entire Koran and to whom The Unseen Presence revealed all His secrets, we can think of Shakespeare as the Hafez of his age who was a diviner in his own right. For centuries our good Muslim folks have been seeking solace in Hafez's *ghazals* whenever misfortunes befell them. As you know, they supplicate Hafez with closed eyes, in the same way they call upon a saint, and open his *divan* of *ghazals* at any page and read the *ghazal* that will show them the way out of their adversities. Now, in my humble opinion, what we should do is to consult Shakespeare so that he can guide us out of this morass by opening the script at random."

How very typical of Iranians, I thought, to treat their greatest poet like this. Instead of reading him at any time just for the pleasure of reading poetry, they only pick his *divan* up, kiss it as they kiss a sacred book, and consult him to see what he says about their difficulties. These might range from suffering brought about by an unrequited love, being burdened with mountains of debt, entering into a risky enterprise, and similar calamities.

"If you could kindly let me have the script," Ostaad Safihollah asked me. I handed it to him.

"I request Sheikh-ol-eslam Pashmeddin to honour us with consulting Shakespeare by performing a divination." Ostaad Safihollah respectfully handed the script to the

71

minister, who grabbed it, closed his eyes and began in a mournful voice to recite the usual formula declaimed when people consult Hafez:

"Oh, Master *Shekespir* of Arabia, I beseech you for the love of your sweetheart to help us to show our brothers here present as how to perform the *daraam* of *Atoghloo* in the best possible Islamic manner."

Upon finding a page at random, he began to read out loud with feeling:

"*In sleep I heard him say, 'Sweet Desdanana,'*"

"Forgive me, Jenaab-e Minister, it is Desdemona," Ostaad Safihoddin politely corrected him.

"That's what I said."

"Right you are," Ostaad Safihollah said apologetically, nervously rubbing his hands together. "Forgive me, I didn't hear you correctly."

"Where was I?" the minister grumbled and continued, "*In sleep I heard him say, 'Sweet Desdanana, Let us be wary, let us hide our loves'*" He raised his eyes from the text and said to me, "I can't make head nor tail of this, brother director. Are these two characters lawfully married or not?"

"Here Iago is recounting to Othello what Cassio was mumbling in his dream about Desdemona," I explained.

"Curse be upon the Satan who makes us dream of such sinful acts," Sayyed Pashmeddin muttered. He adjusted his glasses and carried on reading:

"*And then, sir, would he grip and wring my hand, /Cry 'O sweet creature!' then kiss me hard ...*"

Sayyed Pashmeddin stopped again, tossed the script on the table and groaned loudly.

"This is scandalous. As you know, we men of turban discuss everything under the sun, but '*O sweet creature!*'?"

"*Hazrat-e Hojjat-ol eslam.*" Ostaad Safihollah had to intervene to clarify things further. "Shakespeare has used '*O sweet creature*' as a figure of speech. In the same manner that Hafez has employed many mystical and divine metaphors. In one of his verses, to cite but one example, he says:

Pardon me if the string of my prayer beads was snapped,
I was caressing the silver-white arm of the cup-bearer.

"Here, the silver-white arm of the sweetheart is a metaphorical allusion to divine grace."

"So, all this is nothing but a skilful use of mystical metaphors used by our brother *Shekespir*?" Sayyed Pashmeddin shook his head thoughtfully.

"That's correct, *Hojjat-ol eslam*," Ostaad Safihollah confirmed.

"You know best, Ostaad," Sayyed Pashmeddin said half-heartedly and carried on reading. "*Then he kissed me hard,/As if he plucked up kisses by the roots/That grew upon my lips, laid his leg/O'er my thigh, and sigh, and kiss, and then/Cry, cursed fate that gave thee to the Moor!*"

He stopped, looking traumatised, like a simpleton who has just seen that dream in action before his eyes. He glanced at the two ostaads and growled, "Anyone with a little knowledge of Islamic mysticism can tell you that no mystical allegories can be perceived in this filthy and totally depraved scene. *Baba jaan*, we all know that there are different types of kissing – friends kissing each other's cheeks, brothers and sisters, fathers and children, two sweethearts stealing kisses from each other. But plucking kisses like the ones described in these lines, laying your leg over your bedfellow's thigh, thinking that he is your mistress, albeit in a dream, and groaning meanwhile, are blatantly dissolute and utterly anti-Islamic to even dream about. Just imagine how a decent Muslim audience, in a dark auditorium, would react listening to this lewdness related by that man (he pointed his finger at Iago) on the stage. Kissing means kissing, I say, and don't go on attributing to it some mystical meanings. May I use this opportunity to remind you that Ostaad Jaahelottabaar in his *Encyclopaedia of Mystical Terms* clearly defines that kissing is not a metaphor for any spiritual notions and simply means what it is."

He threw the script on the table, scowled like a grumpy gorilla, and began to bead his rosary furiously, mumbling some curses in Arabic, like the mollah he was.

A deathly silence reigned on the stage. Things did not look good. Through bitter experience and knowledge of past and recent history, I knew that a mollah's anger bodes very ill, especially when he has arrogated to himself the ultimate power of residing over the destiny of artists, poets and writers. Ostaad Safihollah was the one who, once again, dared to break the silence.

"*Jenaab-e Hojjat-ol eslam*," he said apologetically, "I beg of you not to lose your composure over such matters for which solutions can easily be found. Taking back my ill-considered suggestion, may I suggest that our brother actors rehearse a piece from the end of the play?"

"I have no objection," the minister muttered. "Let's start from the end."

"Counting backwards is customary practice by mathematicians and scientists." Ostaad Honarkhor appeared to feel a compulsion to say whatever came to his mind to support the minister's views.

"All right, friends ..." I said, addressing the actors and actresses.

"Friends, no friends!" the guard yelled at me. "These words are used by the communists. You must say brothers and sisters."

"Sorry, brother," I said, grinning nervously. "Brothers and sisters, we can now rehearse a piece from the end of the play."

"And we'll work our way back in reverse gear till we reach the beginning of it," Othello commented.

"Brother Othello," Ostaad Honarkhor said, standing up, "let's not lose sight of the fact that the structure of Islamic drama is inspired by true spirituality and absolute insight bestowed on us by the ideals of the Islamic Revolution. Put simply, it means that we should find out what the pit of a peach looks, smells, and tastes like, before we set upon eating the peach itself."

"As far as I know, we first eat the peach and throw the pit away," Othello said. "Only children, out of curiosity, smash the shell of the pit, taste the seed inside, find it bitter and spit it out."

"Revolutionary art, Brother Othello," Ostaad Honarkhor elucidated, "should, first and foremost, pay attention to the hidden ideological and political core of any sort of art. The edible flesh of the peach has no bearing on the matter." He then grabbed his book, frantically leafed through it, found the relevant page and said, "I have explained clearly here on page 90 of my book that we should ignore all of a writer's words if they are not employed to lead us to the core of his writing. What do I mean by that? Well, I'll tell you. This concealed core is similar to the pit of the peach I referred to earlier – the ideological and political pit of the issues the writer is trying to convey to us."

"So the peach exists only for its pit," Othello said, "and has no other value or benefit?"

Having had enough of Othello relentlessly picking holes in his dubious theories, Ostaad Honarkhor appeared to have run out of ideas. He had now no choice but to resort to the last weapon in his intellectual armoury – suppressing the adversary by calling upon the brute forces at his service provided for him by the all-powerful ayatollahs who in turn followed in the steps of their glorious Arab forebears.

"Please, brother guard," he called out, "can you tell him to be silent, otherwise …"

"Shut your gob and let brother Ostaad say what he has to say," the guard barked at Othello, who fell silent, eyeing the guard like a hunted beast.

"Since all the stories originate from the Koran," Ostaad Honarkhor went on haranguing us unchallenged, "and all the subsequent dramas, such as *ta'zieh* and acting out the stories of the Islamic martyrs using icons, are Islamic arts, therefore, we should dispose of all forms of art that go against the laws set out in our eternal Islamic Sharia. Do you comprehend now what I'm getting at?"

"No, I don't," Othello said, his defiance unabated.

At this point Ostaad Safihollah, true to his nature as an arbitrator, stood up and moved his stretched-out hands, palms downwards, inviting the quarrelsome parties to be calm.

"Allow me, please, if I may, to make a brief explanation," he said in his conciliatory voice. "In *Alsaafaat* Chapter, I think verse six, in the Koran it states: 'We adorned the firmament with stars.'" In this verse Allah the Almighty Himself has revealed to us mortals what in truth Islamic aesthetics signify. According to the Koranic aesthetic, scholarly and perceptively interpreted by Ostaad Honarkhor, in committed Islamic art the glittering stars in heavens are indeed the pits of peaches in their countless numbers, telling us something about the hidden meanings of Allah's creation."

"If those stars are pits of so many peaches," Othello started again, bent on not letting these ostaads off the hook, "where are the branches of the peach trees? If you cannot explain away the absence of trees, then some creatures, maybe aliens, must've eaten the peaches and chucked them into space billions of years ago ..."

"If you don't shut up," the guard snarled at him, "I'll have to call my brothers in the *Monkaraat* to come and drag you away like a dog."

I regarded Othello in despair. He got the message and agreed to keep quiet.

"Forgive me, Ostaad." I turned to Ostaad Safihollah. "If you don't mind, try to make your much-appreciated guidance a bit brief."

"I have no more to say, brother director," he replied. "Except that I wholeheartedly go along with Ostaad Honarkhor's idea of counting backwards."

Hearing this, I turned to the cast.

"Sisters and ... pardon me, I mean brothers and sisters, let's rehearse the last part so that, *inshallah*, with the licence that is granted to us, we will rehearse the play and prepare it for the *mise en scène*."

"What *zonsen*?" the guard rapped out.

"*Mise en scène*, brother," I repeated, trying to stay calm.

"Brother director means that they don't just sit there, but get up and get into action and get moving." Ostaad Safihollah, peacemaker as usual, came to my rescue without realising that he'd made things worse.

"To get moving!" the guard bawled out. "Are they planning a protest march or a demonstration?"

"No, no, brother guard." Ostaad Safihollah hastened to clarify. "You got it wrong. *Mise en scène* means to put on the stage, where actors act, move around, and recite their lines."

"I don't know what you're on about, Ostaad," the guard said, fiddling with his Kalashnikov. "All I know is that Haaj Ghassaal in the *Monkaraat* has ordered us to be on the lookout for any signs of ..."

"Don't you worry, brother." The minister had to intervene. "I will have a word with Haaj Ghassaal and explain everything to him."

"Shall we now get on with the rehearsal, Ostaads?"

"It's about time!" Othello said.

"Now you're talking, brother Othello," Ostaad Honarkhor agreed with obvious relief. "We must definitely crack on with the rehearsal."

"We'll be on it right away," I said. Addressing the actors and actresses, I told them that we were going to rehearse some parts of Act 5, Scene 2 at the end of the drama. I then asked Desdemona to go and lie down on the makeshift bed and pretend that she was deeply asleep.

"Brother Othello," I told him, "you may start, when ready, saying your lines while standing beside

Desdemona's bed. Remember to keep your composure and imagine that you're acting for a real audience."

"Whatever you say," Othello replied. Grabbing a candle, he assumed the right posture, walked gingerly to his wife's bed, and recited in a melancholy voice:

> *It is the cause, it is the cause, my soul:*
> *Let me not name it to you, you chaste stars:*
> *It is the cause. Yet I'll not shed her blood,*
> *Nor scar that whiter skin of hers than snow,*
> *And smooth as monumental alabaster:*
> *Yet she must die, else she'll betray more men.*

"Hold it there!" Ostaad Honarkhor called out. "*Hazrat-e Hojjat-ol-eslam*, what do you make of this, so far?" he asked the minister.

"*Vallah*," the Minister sighed, throwing up his hands in despair, "I cannot make head nor tale of it."

"This woman has been unfaithful to her husband," Ostaad Safihollah explained to him, pointing at Desdemona. "Her husband, brother Othello, is about to take her life."

"Could you repeat that once again?" the minister asked Othello.

"*It is the cause, it is the cause, my soul: / Let me ...*"

"I understood this bit. Just repeat the last lines."

"*Yet I'll not shed her blood, /Nor scar that whiter skin of hers than snow, /And smooth as monumental alabaster:/Yet she must die ...*" Othello recited in a flat, undramatic tone, becoming more and more flustered.

"Well done, brother Othello. Yes, she MUST die." Sayed Pashmeddin bellowed so loudly that Desdemona was startled out of her pretend sleep and sat up.

He then stood up, wrapped his *abaa* round him, pushed past Ostaad Safihollah and strode to the centre of the stage.

"As I had the good fortune to act in several *ta'ziehs* in my native village before taking up my present ministerial duties, I can show you the correct and more Islamic way of acting and declaiming those lines of a husband whose honour is trampled upon by a shameless, adulterous woman."

He lifted the right corner of his *abaa*, tucked it into the left pocket of his *ghabaa*, took on an epic-heroic pose, frowned, twiddled one tip of his moustache with his fingers, then the other, and roared, "In the name of Allah who is merciful to his pious creatures and vengeful to his sinful ones."

He then drew out an imaginary scimitar from its non-existent scabbard, brandished it, swung round on his heels, faced the terrified Desdemona, and, as if acting out the role of a dishonoured Islamic hero in a *ta'zieh*, thundered,

> *Ahoy, is this whore still alive?*
> *Her blood must be spilt without a fear.*
> *To protect the testicles of our Islam,*
> *Kill her in the name of holy Sharia.*

As he menacingly approached Desdemona, she stood up and took refuge behind Othello, who himself was in a state of shock.

Once Sayyed Pashmeddin had finished his Islamic theatricals, he stopped, glared around the stage and took out the corner of his *abaa* from the pocket of his *ghabaa*. All eyes were fixed on him in absolute awe. After reverting to his ministerial self, he calmly asked the two ostaads, "What do the learned ostaads think about my way of acting as an insulted Muslim husband?"

"I have talked, in my numerous researches, exactly about this sort of language that a betrayed husband should use," Ostaad Honarkhor agreed at once.

"I hope you will forgive me," Sayyed Pashmeddin said apologetically, "I'm getting on in years and I don't have the powerful voice I used to have. When I roared like a lion the entire audience in the village square trembled." After settling down on his chair, he said, "Now we have to find out how this woman is going to die."

"Brother Othello," I asked, "could you please recite that bit about *namaaz*."

"*Namaaz!*" Othello gestured to me, not understanding what I meant.

"Yes, *namaaz*," I repeated. "I mean the bit when you ask Desdemona if she's prayed before you take her life."

Othello and Desdemona looked mutely at one another. She walked to the bed and sat on its edge, pulled her scarf down to her brow, smoothed her ruffled hijab, and fell into deep thought.

"*Have you prayed tonight, Desdemona?*" Othello asked gloomily, gazing at the floor.

"*Aye, my lord,*" she replied, also looking down at the floor.

"I hope your *namaaz* will be accepted by Allah who, in His infinite compassion, will decide whether or not to forget your sins when you are awaiting your final fate in purgatory." Sayyed Pashmeddin sounded like one of those mollahs who recite verses of the Koran while squatting beside the graves of departed souls.

"*If you bethink yourself of any crime/Unreconciled as yet to heaven and grace, /Solicit for it straight.*" Othello carried on declaiming.

"Don't these cross-worshippers plead for absolution after performing their *namaaz*?" Sayyed Pashmeddin enquired.

"Sinners like these don't understand such things," the guard brayed out.

At this point the black-clad ghoul-like man reappeared in the hall, climbed up to the stage and looked at the minister, pointing to his watch like a deaf-and-dumb mute. Upon a nod from the minister, he crept meekly down the steps and vanished into the shadows at the back of the hall.

"Brothers and sisters," the minister said, "whatever you want to show us, please make it brief as I have to attend an urgent cabinet meeting concerning the sending of troops to the war front."

I asked Othello and Desdemona to quickly rehearse the murder scene. Othello assumed his vengeful pose, and started to approach Desdemona who, terror-stricken, backed away from him.

"*By heaven, I saw my handkerchief in's hand,*" Othello declaimed angrily.

"If he says he's seen it, he's seen it." The guard cut in to support Othello, for whom he evidently felt a sudden surge of brotherly empathy.

Othello and Desdemona stopped, not knowing what to do next.

"I do not think the use of the handkerchief is appropriate in this context," the minister opined, standing up. "The handkerchief has different connotations according to all Islamic scholars, past and present. A scarf could mean hankie, headdress, or a colourful bandana, depending who you are and what you are doing with it at any place or point in time. In this scene, because the adulterous woman is a practising Christian who's performing her *namaaz*, she has, no doubt, given her prayer mat as a present to her lover Caas … whatever his name is."

"Brother Cassio," Ostaad Safihollah corrected.

"Yes, that's right, brother *Caassiho*."

"By heaven, I saw my prayer mat which I had given you in Cassio's hand." Othello repeated the line loudly, adapting it to the circumstances of the time and place.

"No, no, no," Ostaad Honarkhor said, standing up. "Now that you've changed the handkerchief to a prayer mat, you'll have to stick appropriately to the rules of drama. I don't think you walk around holding your prayer mat in your hand. You sit on it while you're performing your *namaaz*."

"By heaven, I saw with my own eyes Cassio performing his namaaz on the prayer mat I gave you," Othello thundered like an outraged Arab Muslim, averting his eyes from his unrighteous wife. Fed up with this farce, Desdemona just listened, no more in her role, mockingly nodding her head.

"I warned you against these penitents whom we should never let out of our sight," the minister yelled, pointing at Cassio. "First, they commit the cardinal sin of adultery. Next, they perform *namaaz* on the prayer mat desecrated by an adulterous woman."

To show how outraged he was, he looked away and pretended to spit on the floor.

"Hojjat-ol-eslam," Ostaad Safihollah suggested, once again trying to cool down a potentially inflammable situation, "this part could be of immense benefit for our

holy revolution by the skilful way by which we can expose the two-faced anti-revolutionaries."

"I think you have a point there, ostaad," the minister agreed, calming down a bit. "Let's see what happens next."

"Cut it short, please," I told Othello and Desdemona.

"*Kill me tomorrow*," Desdemona pleaded with Othello as he approached her, revenge in his eyes.

"*Nay, an' you strive …*" Othello replied, clutching her neck in his hands.

"*But half an hour! While I say one prayer*," Desdemona implored.

"*It is too late*," Othello answered, trying to strangle her.

"Hold it there, brother!" Sayyed Pashmeddin called out. "The adulterous woman must pay for her sinful acts in accordance with Sharia Law. This is because her husband may be destitute, therefore unable to pay blood money to her relatives. In the Islamic punishment bill – meted out to sinners and criminals according to the law of retaliation – the adulterous woman must be stoned to death."

"Stoned to death!" Desdemona cried, horrified. I gestured to her to calm down.

"Yes, sister," Sayyed Pashmeddin affirmed almost affably. "This is clearly stipulated in the punishment bill of the Islamic Republic."

"Here on the stage?" Desdemona shouted and started to walk towards the minister.

"Where else, woman?" Sayyed Pashmeddin said. "The audience should witness the punishment and learn so that they will not even dream of committing such immoral acts."

"But I haven't …" Desdemona shrieked, red-cheeked with rage. "Listen, you son of a …"

"Sister Desdemona." I had to stop her before she made matters much worse for herself. "I promise I'll sort this problem out when we come to the *mise en scène*."

"But I haven't done anything wrong," Desdemona insisted loudly and planted herself in front of the table where the minister sat.

"No need to be so upset, sister," Sayyed Pashmeddin said in a magnanimous tone. "If it's proved by our expert Islamic judges that you have committed a sin, well, you will pay dearly for your shameful deeds. And if, on the other hand, they find you innocent, you will be rewarded, *inshallah*, by Allah the Most Compassionate. You will have, in paradise, as your companions, not only the Islamic martyrs, but also the most handsome young men called *ghelmans* with whom you can live in absolute bliss till eternity." Pausing so that she could take this in, he stood up and bellowed like a rabble-rouser mollah in a mosque trying to stir vengeful feelings in the mob, "We will kill the infidels and the sinners who stand in the path of our beloved Islam."

Terrified, Desdemona turned and walked rapidly back to her place on the stage, where she stood as quiet as a mouse. One more word from her would have landed her in serious hot water.

Satisfied with his performance as a true Muslim, Sayyed Pashmeddin sat down and fell into a brooding silence. We all dumbly regarded each other, not knowing what to make of the sudden display of Islamic bravado by the minister.

"I am pleased that the adulterous woman will be dealt with very soon in the proper Islamic manner," Sayyed Pashmeddin said, coming back to life. "*Inshallah*, this will provide a lesson to all women."

He rose with difficulty from his chair, wrapped his *abaa* round his fat body, ready to leave. Seeing this, Ostaad Honarkhor also stood up and picked up his briefcase. At this moment Ostaad Safihollah also rose, gently touched the hem of the minister's *abaa* and said, "Haaj Agha, could you please be kind enough to watch this part before we leave. We still have some time left."

"If you wish," the minister said. "As long as it is not too long."

Ostaad Safihollah asked me if brother Othello and sister Emilia could rehearse the part when Othello has a tête-à-tête with Emilia. Emilia walked to Othello, who sat down on the platform, acting the betrayed husband.

"'*Tis pitiful; but yet Iago knows/That she with Cassio hath the act of shame/ A thousand times committed. Cassio confessed it ...*" Othello declaimed in a mournful voice.

"We are running out of time." The minister looked at his watch, pointed at Emilia and asked me, "As I recall, I think you said this sister's name was *Omm-e Leyla*?"

"Her name is Emilia, *Hazrat-e Hojjat-ol eslam*," I corrected him.

"That is what the British Imperialists called her," the minister snapped. "When brother *Shekespir* wrote his play for the first time, her name must have been *Omm-e Leyla*, as the play's origins, as Ostaad Honarkhor made it clear to all of us with his commendable scholarship, was an Arabic folk tale. You said that she is the wife of brother *Yaahoo*. Is that so?"

"That's right, Jenaab-e Minister." I nodded, grabbed Iago's arm and pulled him forward.

"May the blessings of Allah be showered upon this married couple," the minister said solemnly.

"What I want to know is that how she will appear as a revolutionary sister in the *daraam*, just like one of our dear Zainab Sisters who sacrificed everything for our unique Islamic Revolution," he demanded.

I walked up to Emilia and asked her to rehearse her revolutionary role at the end of the play. She stood up like an obedient girl, smoothed out her hijab, and tiptoed towards the makeshift bed on which Desdemona was now lying, pretending she was dead.

"What did thy song bode, lady? / Hark, canst thou hear me? I will play the swan, / And die in music: –/ Willow, willow, willow," she declaimed in a heart-rending tone, looking down at the lifeless body of Desdemona and slowly sitting down beside the bed. To accompany this tragic scene I signalled to Cassio to turn on the tape-recorder hidden behind the backdrop. A melancholy music floated in the air.

"I have another weapon in this chamber; / It is a sword of Spain, the ice-brook's temper," Othello declaimed in a voice choked with thoughts of revenge.

"I totally object," Ostaad Honarkhor shouted, jumping to his feet and making Emilia start. "Only anti-revolutionaries use this kind of language to communicate in codes imbedded in songs and anthems. *Canst thou hear* is a sort of code. *The weapon in the brook* is a coded allusion to a possible guerrilla or secret operation being hatched somewhere by communists and secret agents who work for the Great Satan against the Islamic Republic."

"These lines were written several centuries ago," Othello said wearily, by now resigned to hearing yet more nonsense. He stood up, took a few steps towards the minister and said, "What have they to do with guerrilla or secret agents' operations?"

"The seeds of animosity against our beloved Islam, as Imam Khomeini has emphasised over and over again, were sown in those days by our mortal enemies," Sayyed Pashmeddin screeched, raising his hand. He went on heatedly, now raising himself halfway, now sitting down, gesticulating like a disjointed marionette, and spluttering all over his beard. "These communists and hypocrites are much worse than the infidels and pagans Prophet Mohammad had to deal with at the dawn of Islam. The Great Satan was always there, from everlasting to everlasting. The Great Satan has been and is behind all these ideas and practices such as the passing of ..." He turned to Ostaad Safihollah and asked, "What was it that they pass to one another?"

"Code."

"That's right, *coat*," he repeated.

"That means the passing of secret messages to spies and enemies of Islam using coded language," Ostaad Safihollah explained.

"No, Agha Director." Sayyed Pashmeddin took up the thread of his sermon, fuming like a hairy mad bull. "This *daraam*, written by Agha *Atoghloo*, which you have tried hard to transform into an Islamic one, is influenced by cultural imperialism, and I can go as far as to say that it has even been tampered with by the International Zionist Front who stick their filthy noses into everything."

"Haaj Agha," the guard bawled out without warning, "allow me to call my brothers in the Nest of Spies to bring all the secret documents about this motherf ..."

"Brother guard," Ostaad Safihollah cut him short halfway through his swearword before he revealed his true character, "the real Othello died during one of his battles a long time ago."

"*Zeki*," the guard barked. "What do you mean he died long time ago? The son of a gun anti-revolutionary is sitting here in flesh and blood and keeps saying that he's *Ottelloo*. I've heard him say this a hundred times. And his documents are all in the Nest of Spies for all to see. The job of the Islamic Revolutionary Court is to line up these Ottelloos, Yaahoos, and Caassihos against the wall and fill them up with bullets. I swear to the Prince of the Martyrs that I would willingly tear their hearts into shreds with the bullets of my Kalashnikov."

Seeing the guard's outburst, Ostaad Safihollah stood up and rushed to him, trying to calm him down. Terrified, I hid behind Ostaad Safihollah in case the guard lost it and pulled the trigger. A lot of fanatical revolutionary guards had, in the past few years, killed many innocent people whom they did not like.

"Brother guard," he said in a pacifying tone, "if you can be patient a little, we will sort things out." After returning to the table he went on, "As Ostaad Honarkhor, no doubt, agrees with me, the play must undergo a complete change. What I mean is that it should be given a divine, spiritual form, which, as our modern Islamic scholars put it, goes beyond the appearance and what is visible to us in a show, becoming united with the grace of Allah. As a result of this metamorphosis the dramatic beauty will take a totally celestial form. This, put simply, means, firstly, to wipe out from the surface of the planet the enemies of Islam. Secondly, to change the content of the play, so that it will be in total harmony with the politico-ideological Islamic doctrine. Thirdly, this will mean that Islam, with all its sublime beauties, will put an end forever to all the misfortunes of the wretched of the earth everywhere."

We listened to this dangerous charade in silence. Othello was the one, once again, who spoke first.

"*Yes, it is unfortunate ..., but ...*" He declaimed one of his lines in the desolate voice of a beaten man.

"*Oh,*" Emilia echoed.

"*Hold your peace,*" Cassio followed.

"*'Twill out; 'twill out! I peace? No, I will speak as liberal as the north,*" Emilia uttered defiantly.

"You dare speak," the guard howled, "and I'll drag you to the Revolutionary Committee."

"*Let heaven and men and devils, let them all, /All, all cry shame against me, yet ...*" Emilia went on with another line.

"Shut your gob, you so-and-so sister!" the guard yelled at her, moving threateningly towards her.

Sensing imminent danger, Emilia and the other actors hurried helter-skelter towards the stage door, followed by Desdemona who thought it would not be wise to remain alone and defenceless on the bed.

The way they grumbled among themselves about the possibility of being taken to the Revolutionary Court, which would mean interrogations and possible imprisonment, I made up my mind to beg them to stay and perform the last act by Othello and Desdemona in the hope of, perhaps, saving something of the play, albeit a grotesquely corrupted version, so that we could stage it for the audience to see for themselves what can happen to a Western drama in the hands of mollahs in the Islamic Republic. All my friends looked at me as if I had lost my marbles. Finally, Othello and Desdemona agreed on one condition, that this would be the last time.

Desdemona walked to the bed and lay down on it, acting as if she were dead, killed by Othello minutes ago.

Othello then disappeared behind the stage and emerged with a lit candle wedged in a candlestick. He warily approached the bed, looked down at Desdemona's dead body and said with a grief-stricken wail:

> *I kissed thee ere I killed thee: no way but this,*
> *Killing myself, to die upon a kiss.*

"No, no, no!" Ostaad Honarkhor called out, startling Desdemona again. "This part of the drama goes against Islamic morality. I beg of Haaj Agha Pashmeddin to express his views."

"I am speechless, brother Honarkhor." Sayyed Pashmeddin threw his hands up in despair, like a humble mollah who has just witnessed a horror of horrors that was about to be performed on the stage. "Our Islamic scholars have written volumes on the shameful subject of necrophilia. Whether you are a married man or a married woman, if you commit such a repulsive crime of engaging in sinful acts of a dissipated nature with a corpse, you will end up in the deepest part of hell in which your skin will be burned by tongues of fire that lash at you from rivers of molten lava. Once you become roasted, your body will be devoured by a gigantic snake that will spew you out over and over again to be roasted and devoured again, till eternity."

Exhausted by his outrage, he fell silent for a moment, fidgeted with his turban and *abaa*, and beaded his rosary frantically, muttering some curses in Arabic.

"No, ostaads," he squealed at the top of his voice, glancing right and left to his mute-as-marionettes aides and waving the manuscript, "it is now very clear to me that this *daraam* written by that *Atoghloo* fellow, even if you have tried to make it look more Islamic, has secret links with global imperialism and even with international Zionism." He stood up, rudely pushed Ostaad Safihollah back, strutted to the middle of the stage, chucked the manuscript in the air, and pointed his threatening finger at all of us, thundering, "These people have shown that they are the sworn enemies of the Islamic Republic and must pay dearly for their deeds."

Seeing this extraordinary show of rage from the normally calm and composed minister, the two ostaads stood up at the same time and followed him like two automatons to the front of the stage.

Sniffing the scent of fresh prey in the vicinity, the hairy beast in human clothes emerged from his lair in the shadows of the hall and joined his revolutionary guard colleague on the stage, ready to follow the commands of the minister to leap upon his victims who, attired in hopelessly ridiculous Shakespearian costumes and Islamic rags, trembled like weeping willows in a chilly wind.

"Listen, brother Bimokh," the minister ordered the gentleman-beast, "can you see to it that these people will remain under the surveillance of your men till we come to an appropriate decision about them." He then addressed the two silent colleagues. "Let's go, ostaads."

Othello and I squatted and began to gather the sheets of the manuscript scattered in the middle of the stage. As I cast a glance back at him, Othello, who looked as if possessed by a demon, was fixing his eyes like a leopard on to the minister, ready to jump at his throat. He then sat on his haunches like an athlete preparing himself for a sprint, and began to declaim in a threatening tone one of his lines, not taking his eyes off the minister.

Soft you; a word or two before you go.

"Bah," the guard scoffed, cutting him short. "Look at him. This *Ottelloo* fellow thinks he's still somebody and can say whatever he likes. The Revolutionary Court will decide about guys like you."

"Brother guard," the minister reminded him, "do not forget that Allah is infinitely merciful and compassionate and leaves the doors of heaven wide open to all of his creatures, even if they commit the most unspeakable crimes. Maybe Allah's inexhaustible grace has touched brother *Atoghloo's* heart, making him regret his sins, beg forgiveness, and be welcomed to the community of the penitents' brotherhood."

Untroubled by the guard's threat and unmoved by the minister's heart-warming words, Othello went on, in the same manner:

I have done the state some service, and they know't –
No more of that. I pray you, in your letters,
When you shall these unlucky deeds relate,
Speak of me as I am: nothing extenuate,
Nor set down aught in malice.

He then rose to his feet, stretched himself to his full height, never taking his eyes off the minister, and declaimed in the tone of a man with no pity for his adversary, some other vengeful lines from the same speech:

And say besides that in Aleppo once,
Where a malignant and a turbaned Turk
Beat a Venetian and traduced the state,
I took by th'throat the circumcised dog
And smote him, thus.

All of a sudden, he jumped forward and snatched Iago's wooden sword from its scabbard, clutched it with both hands, raised it aloft, and charged towards Sayyed Pashmeddin, intending to bring it down with all his might on the turbaned cranium. Before he could hit his target, the guard and the man-beast leapt on him, pinned him down to the floor and prised the sword from his grip, growling like wild boars. The man-beast took his walkie-talkie off his belt and called for help. In a few seconds a pack of bearded men poured into the workshop, pointing their guns at all of us. Freaked out of our wits, we all stood there, unable to make any sense of what was going on. Holding a bundle of manuscript sheets in my hand, I slowly raised myself to my full height, wondering what had come over Othello.

"Take him away, brothers," the minister ordered the guard and the man-beast. "May Allah protect us from these ungodly madmen before they get hold of real weapons."

Several hairy men hustled the minister and his entourage out of the workshop, leaving us with the two men who soon dragged poor Othello off the stage, his wretched nobleman's robe trailing pitifully on the wooden planks.

If you see on your way a severed head
Tumbling along to that square of ours,
Ask it, just ask it, how we all fare;
It will tell you that buried secret of ours!

TRAGEDY

Othello gone, we all stood there on the stage, gazing into nothing, not knowing what to make of this sudden coup de théâtre we had just witnessed. What had happened to Othello (or rather, my good friend Amir)? Why did he lose it like that? Was all that farcical absurdity too much for him to bear? Or did he really believe he had become the latter-day Moorish general who could slay his enemies with the might of his sword, forgetting for an instant that it was merely a wooden one, bought from a toyshop in the Bazaar, to be used for the stage-fighting? Despite the sadness of that out-of-place-and-time heroic deed, I could not help smiling, thinking how the extraordinary events of the day had turned my poor friend into an Iranian Don Quixote, not de la Mancha, but de la Tehran, who had determined to dream the impossible dream of fighting the centuries-old unbeatable foe.

Our dreams of staging a Shakespearian tragedy being shattered, nothing was left for us to do in that sad workshop but to leave it as soon as possible. My friends took off their now ridiculous-looking costumes and Islamic hijabs, shoved them into the gunny-sacks, and put on their everyday clothes. I told them to leave as soon as possible without me, as I needed to stay behind a little longer to sort a few things out. I promised I would catch up with them later.

Once they were gone, I sat on a chair in the front row in the hall and stared at the stage. It looked like a room ransacked by burglars. I had hoped to stage, one day, a great play there. We had been like a bunch of eager schoolkids who, with so much joy in their innocent hearts, wanted to put on an entertaining show in their school. But, as always happens in our glorious homeland, our hopes had been dashed against a colossal wall of ignorance and tyranny. Not being able to bear that deserted workshop, I stood up and left.

Once outside, I felt as if I had come out of a dark cellar to the light of day. I blinked and looked at the people of Tehran, who, insect-like, were scuttling here and there in the mid-afternoon sun, to eke out their wretched livings, ever-mindful of the nightmares coming their way.

As I strolled in the streets of Lalezaar, I kept pondering Amir's fate. How could they treat a man that way who just wanted to do some acting every now and then purely because he was passionate about it? How could they drag away an amateur actor like a mongrel dog, who only used a wooden sword to fight them with? What would happen to Amir now? I dreaded to think about what they were capable of doing to a man like him; a man who cannot keep quiet in the face of tyrannical absurdity. He had always tried doggedly to right the unrightable wrong, to reach the unreachable stars. After walking aimlessly in the streets, I arrived home, and explained what had happened to my wife.

"What are you going to do now, Behrouz?" she asked, worried.

"I'm not going to sit back and do nothing," I said. "I will write article after article about the fate of drama in the Islamic Republic."

From that day on our lives changed completely. The following day we were all summoned to the Revolutionary Court and were given harsh warnings and ordered not to engage in any sort of cultural activities – writing, acting, directing, and so on and so forth. We all signed so-called legally-binding, shit-eating documents and left the building that was heavily guarded by Kalashnikov-hugging, bearded young men.

Our friend Amir had completely vanished, no one knew where. The rest of us, even if we kept a low profile for a while, knew that we were under surveillance by plain-clothes men who were on the lookout on every street corner, sitting idly in their cars, or pretending to be ordinary fellows loitering about our workplaces and where we lived.

One chilly evening in October 1980, Arezoo, good old Desdemona, called me.

"Have you heard the news?" she almost yelled.

"What news?"

"They've let Amir out!"

"Amir!" I repeated. "How do you know he's out?"

"Goudarz just called me," she replied. "He couldn't get hold of you, so he called me."

Late that evening my phone rang and I recognised Amir's voice. He sounded gruff and tired. I asked him if I could see him the following day around midday in Haydar's teahouse in Lalezaar, which used to be our usual haunt before the revolution. I told him to walk through the back streets and lanes so that no one could easily follow him.

Just before noon I arrived at the teahouse, found a bench, ordered a glass of tea, and waited for Amir to arrive. A thick cloud of smoke laden with steam hung in the air. As I sipped my tea, I looked around at the customers. The ones who sat alone popped sugar cubes into their mouths and slurped their teas, preoccupied, no doubt, with gloomy thoughts. Others, who clustered around tables, took hard drags at their cigarettes and talked among themselves in subdued voices. Unlike the old days, the funereal braying of the Koran reciter that poured out of the radio like a curse added to the miserable atmosphere of the teahouse. The noisy, cheerful mood of bygone days was replaced with hushed voices. Haydar, who used to walk round the benches and tables, cracking jokes with the customers, looked tired and aged a little with greying hair and stubble. With a teacloth flung over his shoulder, he stood beside the huge brass samovar on the crown of which a large teapot roosted, whistling away. The samovar spouted a dense steam into the air, making the smoke-filled air even mistier. Haydar, from time to time, called out to the young teaboy, reminding him to attend to the newly-arriving customers.

I lit up a cigarette and kept casting anxious glances at the door. Then I saw Amir, who appeared outside, hesitated a while near the door, cautiously looking this way and that. Certain that no one had followed him there, he stepped inside. I stood up to greet him.

"Amir," I hailed him, beckoning him to come over.

We gave each other a bear hug.

"Good to see that you're safe and sound, mate," I said.

"Good to see you, too, Behrouz," Amir said and sat down.

I asked the tea boy to bring us two freshly brewed teas. I offered Amir a cigarette. He smoked quietly, glancing around thoughtfully. I let him have a few sips of his tea before talking about the many things on our minds.

"Tell me first what happened after you disappeared like that," I asked.

"Nothing much, really."

"You mean nothing happened in the past month?"

"Straight from the workshop I was driven in a car to the Revolutionary Court." Amir began his story. "Some men, smartly-dressed in plain clothes, came in to question me about my motives for my sudden outburst."

"Hmm," I muttered. "Only former members of SAVAK wear smart clothes; the notorious gentlemen-torturers of the Pahlavi Regime."

"You're right, Behrouz," Amir agreed, taking a deep drag at his cigarette. "The lackeys of these mollahs are all bearded, rough-looking lumpen, the scum left by the Shah and his cronies after they fled Iran like rats that abandon a sinking ship, as the likes of them always do in our glorious land. SAVAK agents pretended to be sophisticated by calling each other doctors and engineers, proud that they were trained by the CIA and the Israelis in how to interrogate and torture without leaving too many physical marks on their victims."

"I hope they didn't torture you, Amir," I said guardedly.

"Apart from a few wallops across my face and calling me a motherfucker communist, they had no legitimate reason to torture me," he said.

"Why is that?"

"Because I stayed firmly in my role as Othello." He chuckled.

"Othello!"

"Yes, Othello," he said calmly. "I even looked a bit like the Moorish general as I didn't let them take my robe off me."

"I hope you're not going to say they believed you!"

"They certainly did, eventually."

"Didn't they, sooner or later, find out that you were putting on an act to save your skin?"

"Nope," Amir said. "I just stayed in my role at all times. Even if I was left alone, I talked and acted like the general. Sometimes those morose-looking bastards couldn't help laughing helplessly. They seemed to find the whole affair somewhat amusing."

"Where did you get this ingenious idea?"

"From a soldier friend of mine."

"A soldier!"

"Yes, a soldier," he echoed. "During my military service in Kerman at the time of the Shah this soldier friend, after we'd settled in our barracks upon our arrival, hit upon the brilliant idea of acting as a madman so that he could be exempted, in order not to waste two precious years of his life in a most useless and futile service."

"What did he do?"

"The first night, when the dormitory was plunged into darkness and all the soldiers began to snore and grunt, he climbed down from the bunk bed, tiptoed out of the dormitory, and strutted in the grounds of the barracks, singing and dancing while clicking his fingers. Believing he was taking them for a ride, the officers decided to mete out to him a taste of solitary confinement by shoving him into a dingy little room at the end of the barracks for days on end. As he carried on singing and dancing on his own in that room, causing a lot of embarrassment and worry for the officers, they resorted to more severe punishments. None of them worked. He then stopped shaving his face and refused to go to the weekly bathhouse. Instead of doing his marches in step with the other soldiers in the drilling grounds, he just ran around, dancing and singing at the top of his voice. The officers in charge decided not to take him to the plots of land for shooting practice outside the barracks as he could easily shoot some of them, thinking perhaps he was merely handling a toy gun. The pompous, highest-ranking officers who came to watch our marching performance, found his behaviour very non-martial and effeminate for a disciplined soldier."

"So, what did they do to him in the end?"

"Tired of his tomfoolery, the military authorities finally agreed to refer him to the army doctor, who came to the conclusion that my friend had indeed gone mad and was not fit for military duties."

"And?"

"Nothing," Amir said. "He was soon exempted and kicked out of the barracks, dancing and singing his way to the town, where he took a coach back to Tehran."

"What did he do when he was out?"

"When I was on leave I saw him one day loitering outside a cinema."

"Did he behave like a normal man?"

"He appeared normal enough to me. Only sometimes, he told me, when he found himself alone in a quiet corner of a park or in isolated parts of the mountains where he went rambling, he couldn't help singing and dancing just to amuse his friends."

I couldn't help smiling at his story.

"I suppose those flunkies of the mollahs let you off the hook because they thought they were dealing with a loony who believed himself to be a Moorish general of olden times in Venice."

"Spot on, Behrouz," Amir said. "When, finally, having had enough of my ceaseless lunacy, they came one day to set me free, I even refused to leave the building."

"No way!"

"In order to make my madness look convincing, I insisted, the General Othello that I was, I would only leave my legitimate residence, prison that is, if I had to go out to fight the enemies of the homeland."

"So what happened then?"

"On the advice of the former SAVAK doctor and self-appointed shrink – a relic from the Pahlavi era who was kept in prison to help the prisoners – they assured me that I could be more useful outside my castle by leading the beleaguered army of Islam to a final victory against that son of a bitch, Saddam Hossein."

"Did they take you to the front to fight?"

"Of course not," Amir said. "It would've created a scandal to drop a lunatic into the frontline, asking him to lead an army of incompetent, indoctrinated idiots."

"Have you heard that those poor young soldiers, carted to the front from all over Iran, are actually given gold-plated keys to paradise by the ayatollahs to clear the way by jumping over mines, getting torn to pieces, in order to end up in heaven in the next world?"

"I heard about that while I was in the penitentiary," Amir said, his face clouding over with dark thoughts.

"So what did they do to you after setting you free?" I asked.

"Once I was outside the prison, they just abandoned me and disappeared back inside."

"I stood there for a while in my clownish robe. In order to appear an authentic loony, I tried to enter the prison and asked them to take me to the front to fight. The sentry soldiers shoved me back and told to me to piss off. I hung around beside the prison gate for a while. A mob of anxious-looking visitors, who were going in and out of the prison, stood for a minute or two and eyed me up and down, thinking that I was, in all likelihood, a street entertainer of some sort, mimicking an old Persian king.

"Making sure that no one bothered about me, having achieved what I wanted, I began to stroll down the streets and alleyways. As I didn't have any money on me, I walked all the way to Goudarz's flat, which was the closest to the prison. I rang the bell, but no one was in. I sat on the edge of the ditch in the middle of the lane and waited. The passers-by, thinking that I was an entertainer having a bit of a rest, cast curious glances at me and went on their way. It was late afternoon when Goudarz showed up. He was totally shocked to see me there still in my Othello get-up. I explained everything to him. He listened with disbelief and laughed helplessly. Once inside his flat, over a few glasses of tea, we smoked and talked about the latest developments concerning the so-called bloody Cultural Revolution and the war that was raging between the Ayatollahs and Saddam Hossein. Then I called Arezoo and told her about my release. I changed into ordinary clothes that Goudarz lent me and we went to see my landlord to get a spare key for my flat. As soon as I was in my flat I contacted you."

Amir stopped talking. The teahouse was now packed with customers who were having their lunch, as silent as convicts in a smoke-filled dungeon.

"Before we go, Amir," I said, "I've been burning to ask you one question."

"What's that?"

"I had been thinking hard to understand your bizarre behaviour that day in the workshop when you grabbed Cassio's wooden sword and charged at that minister," I said. "What the hell happened to you all of a sudden? Why did you go so dangerously berserk like that?"

"You see, Behrouz," Amir replied, "I've been trying to work that out myself. All I recall is that something snapped in me. As if all the insanities that were going on in our country combined with the absurdities we experienced in the workshop shoved me through the flimsy threshold that separates rational behaviour from the irrational."

"So what you're saying is that you just did it without being conscious of it?"

"At the time, yes."

"I suppose all became clear later as to why you did it?"

"As soon as they started dragging me out of the workshop, it dawned on me what a dangerous fix I'd got myself into by that crazy outburst."

"Were you scared what they might do to you after such a flare-up, especially these days?"

"The hell I was," Amir replied. "No one in his right mind consciously plans to end up in the hands of those motherfuckers."

"Now I understand why you remained in your role as Othello."

"That's right," he said. "From the moment they shoved me into the car I thought I'd better keep play-acting to save my skin. I went on declaiming some of Othello's lines in the car, reminding them of my countless military accomplishments in the battlefield."

I gave a sardonic smile.

"I know, I know," Amir said, chuckling. "The whole thing is the stuff of a good comedy, isn't it?"

"It is, mate, it is," I agreed thoughtfully. "But more like a great tragi-comedy, I'd say."

"Come to think of it, I can see your point there," Amir said. "Just imagine trying to break lance with such a deeply-entrenched adversary using a wooden sword!"

"Even if you'd had a real one, mate, you wouldn't have been able to cut through the many folds of well-wrapped turban to reach the minister's skull!" I said. "Those motherfuckers are far more clever than we think. Only a samurai sword could slice through those bloody turbans!"

"You're damn right, Behrouz." A wry smile flitted across Amir's lips. "The problem is that even if you manage to send one of them to hell, another will immediately take his place. They're like good old Kerman carpets: the more you tread on them, the more precious and durable they become."

"All things considered," I said, "one can read something profound into your action that day. That wooden sword could be a symbol of the futile struggle of our enlightened men and women who are left with nothing else to fight with. When we hit the bottom of the pit of despair, we resort to anything, absolutely anything. We hark back to the primitive means of our ancestors and use anything at our disposal: stones, sticks, slingshots, tearing ourselves into pieces by suicide bombing, and, finally, hostage-taking. And if they don't work, we curse, we swear, we scream Allah-o Akbar, death to America, death to Britain, death to Israel. As if by wishing them death they'll all vanish from the surface of this planet."

We sat there occupied with these grim thoughts. It was well past midday and some customers had left the teahouse. Amir and I decided that it was time for us to go about our business. We said goodbye and promised to keep in touch.

Whenever I saw my friends we would talk about the catastrophic direction art and literature, particularly drama, had taken in those days. The regime of the ayatollahs was spreading its tentacles rapidly in all aspects of Iranian life, snuffing out all voices of dissent. We had all experienced, in the past few months, how hopeless the situation was becoming. Street thugs, supported and financed by the mollahs, roamed everywhere like hordes of barbarians, attacking all cultural gatherings, beating up men and women of culture, and smashing the furniture. Many actors, film-makers, writers, poets, and musicians had left Iran, or were planning to leave the country of their ancestors which they loved so much; the country that also had betrayed them on many occasions, both in the past and now the present.

Tired of discussing these depressing subjects, we began to talk about the past and our passion for all things dramatic.

"If only we could at least have staged *Othello*," I brought up that painful subject one night, "it would've been quite something."

"We all know that it didn't work, Behrouz," Arezoo said sadly.

"No, no, what I really mean is that we should've gone along with the minister's advice and staged the Islamic version of the play."

"The Islamic version!" They all regarded me as if I had gone bonkers.

"Yes, the Islamic version," I repeated. "You see, the Islamic version would've become absolutely hilarious, exposing the archaic notions of these idiots who are stuck at the dawn of Islam in the Arabic Peninsula."

"I can see your point, Behrouz," Jahaangir said, chuckling. "I cannot even imagine what grotesque monstrosity that great tragedy would've been transformed into."

"A farcical travesty of that great tragedy, for sure," Faraanak said.

"That would've been something to watch and have a good laugh, at least," Goudarz agreed. "Particularly for people who have seen the real version. The contrast would've been something to wonder about."

That night was the last we were all gathered together.

After that day we were all tossed about, like debris from a shipwreck, in different directions by the unrelenting waves of the Islamic Revolution. Fearful of being arrested and having no time to see each other much due to family commitments and our daily struggles to survive, we were left alone, doing all sorts of precarious jobs to eke out a living for ourselves and our families. Jahaangir and Amir were the only ones who never abandoned their passion for drama, each after his own fashion. Jahangir, even if he was meted out generous thrashings by Hezbollahi thugs for staging some short plays in abandoned workshops or derelict warehouses in downtown Tehran, resorted to staging topical plays by young playwrights on the rooftops or even in the mountains north of Tehran. I heard that, to escape the brutal suppressive machine of the regime, other famous storytellers, musicians, and entertainers were doing the same.

Finding it impossible to remain quiet in the face of the unfolding calamity, I continued writing articles about the importance of staging all types of drama without government restrictions in some newspapers that had managed, using all the tricks they could think of, to dodge the ever-spreading plague of censorship. As for Amir, he kept in touch with me less and less, his excuse being that he was doing odd jobs to keep his family going.

One day I had some business to attend to midtown. As I was approaching the Nasr Theatre, I saw a throng of idle folk crowding around a man who was performing some sort of street entertainment. Curious, I stood on the edge of the crowd, stretched my neck and, to my surprise, I recognised Amir, who had made himself look like Othello by wearing his shabby robe, reciting some of his lines in an overdramatic manner. After Shakespeare he began to recite some lines from other playwrights. At first, I did not know what to make of this. Why was he doing it? Was it for money? Or was it because he had lost it? Maybe he wanted to prove to the undercover agents, who were now crawling everywhere, that he was still the Moorish general. Hard to tell. When he finished his performance, a few bystanders dropped some coins in a hat placed in front of him on the pavement. He then collected the coins from his hat, took off his robe and moved on, the devil knows to which part of Tehran. Something stopped me from following and maybe questioning him. I could not bear to embarrass that proud friend of mine. When I saw him a few times in some of the bookshops opposite the University of Tehran, I never mentioned anything about his Shakespearean antics on Tehran's pavements and he kept quiet about his on-the-sly dramatic performances, for whatever reason.

Well, one could never know for sure what people were up to during those days of never-seen-before social and cultural turmoil in our history. Those powerful convulsions in a still deeply religious, ignorant, and largely illiterate society, despite what the Shah had made the people believe, had jolted them to the core of their existence. They were running around here and there like lunatics in a loony bin, who had gone berserk upon hearing a very loud explosion, some shrieking, some huddling together for comfort, others banging their heads against the walls and tree trunks, some even singing and dancing. People were not able to keep up with the fast-moving events and the non-stop imposition of suppressive rules and decrees relentlessly crashing down on their heads. The word 'tomorrow' and the future were pregnant with unknown, terrifying monsters, lurking in every corner to pounce. One had no idea what was going to happen when one woke up in the morning. The air was foul with anxiety and fear – fear of losing everything one held dear, fear of that dreadful knock on the door at dawn, fear of being arrested without having committed any crime, fear of being betrayed by one's closest friends, let alone lifelong enemies, fear of one's teenage children being taken away from school to unknown places to be interrogated about their parents' activities and beliefs, following Imam Khomeini's edicts.

Like their forefathers at the dawn of Islam who turned Iran into a slaughterhouse, no symbol of civilisation escaped the destructive onslaught of the mollahs. Among all these symbols of Western decadence were the cinemas and theatres. Hordes of Hezbollahi thugs raided the cinemas, smashed the chairs, ransacked the film archives, and set fire to the billboards, through the charred façade of which one could still see the soot-covered pictures of actors in their manly poses and dancing, half-naked actresses, all frozen in time. All the theatres were shut down, except a handful that toed the revolutionary line, showing tasteless plays.

Some of the first casualties, among countless others, were the former actors and actresses. Soon after the revolution they were all summoned to the Revolutionary Court to be told that they were banned from engaging in any artistic activities. Having lost their career, a number of them found ordinary jobs, leading ordinary lives, and were lost somewhere in that whorehouse of a city called Tehran, soon joined by the forgotten artists, poets, and writers in that land of glory. The lucky ones managed to flee their homeland. The unlucky ones had to beg hand-to-mouth for their daily bread, handful of tea, sugar cubes, cigarettes and sandwiches from struggling charitable organisations. Once the funds of these precarious bodies dried up, many of these wretched souls ended up in abject poverty. Some quick-witted ones, out of sheer despair, resorted to entertaining Tehranis during wedding ceremonies or circumcision parties for measly cash. Some others became street entertainers, wandering all over the city, selling their out-of-time-and-place talents. The more desperate ones managed to scrape a living by taking up the roles of former SAVAK agents, anti-revolutionaries, and revolutionary guards in plays staged in some of the popular theatres approved by the mollahs, in the Lalezaar district of Tehran. This is why it would not have surprised me if my friend Amir had gone crazy, as so many formerly respectable men and women from all walks of life, having lost everything that gave meaning to their existence, had gone insane, doing bizarre things.

I will never forget the case of a famous actress, poet, and writer who was ordered by the Revolutionary Court to stop acting because she had danced half-naked in some films during the Pahlavi era. Overnight her life was turned upside-down. As happens in our glorious land, people quickly forget who you once were as soon as you fall through the cracks due to either personal afflictions or social catastrophes. No one showed a bit of interest in her books of poetry or her short stories, or even the short film she directed – the first female to have done so – just before the revolution. Soon she was left with not even two *tomans* to buy two meters of shroud for herself. Some people are condemned to live, as the saying goes, only because they are not able to afford a piece of shroud.

She was not able to leave Iran in order to lead an uncertain existence in exile, as the lucky ones had. Being kicked out of her rented hovel in a lodging-house, she ended up as a bag-lady, sleeping rough in parks, graveyards, the courtyards of holy shrines, and public toilets. A friend of mine had seen her one day, ambling in her worn-out shoes and tattered rags outside some burnt-down cinemas in Soraya Square, stopping passers-by and telling them that once she was a bit of a celebrity, whose films were shown in those cinemas. My friend, having read some of her poems and seen most of the films she had played in, had just about managed to recognise her. She had changed so much that no one could see the fresh-faced, beautiful woman she once was beyond that ravaged, meaty face.

In order to keep my sanity I had to fight back, whatever the cost. My way of doing this was to write articles in some struggling-to-survive newspapers. I also wrote a number of plays in the vain hope that one day the dark clouds hanging over our country would be cleared away by fresh winds so that I would be able to stage them. As the days and weeks came and went, it dawned on me that I was deluding myself. The mollahs were here to stay, digging themselves deeper and deeper into all aspects of Iranian culture. They had grabbed the reins of the sick and dying nags pulling the rickety funereal hearse on which was placed the coffin of our nation, hurtling towards the deepest and darkest of all abysses. Radical and real change will never come to any nation if the individuals who make up that nation are not willing to become the embodiment of change.

The regime of mollahs, faithful to their Arab ancestors, after silencing all political parties and cultural groups, started to persecute journalists, writers, and poets of all political denominations, except the ones who sang, praised, and fondled the balls of the supreme leader and his lackeys. Having a good knowledge of my background at the time of the Pahlavi regime, due to the records kept by SAVAK, the new regime started to ask me, in a reasonably respectable manner, to keep quiet. I ignored them and went on writing my harshly critical articles. They began to offer me all sorts of rewards if I changed my views and wrote for them, praising Islam and the still unripe fruits of the Islamic Revolution. Refusing to collaborate, I went on with my protest. Having failed to lure me into their camp, unlike so many writers who had joined them, they resorted to the tactics of threats and warnings in the time-honoured tradition of Iranian strongmen and knife-fighters.

No sooner had I published an article in the only surviving opposition paper than the office phones rang, with someone spewing out foul swearwords, like pestilence, on the chief editor, myself, and our poor mothers, of course. As these threats became more frequent and extreme, some of my friends advised me not to stay at my own address as the mad dogs of the regime had been unleashed, prowling in the streets, alleyways and lanes, sniffing around the homes of dissident journalists to find them and drag them out, and send them to a place from where no man or a woman had ever returned alive. By the time my friends had made secret arrangements to find somewhere for me to hide, the regime's killers had already imprisoned a few of my journalist friends.

The supreme leader, Imam Khomeini, his brain completely infested by Islamic ideology, had now gone bloodthirsty, howling in his daily sermons like a hungry wild beast, ordering his packs of hyenas to hunt for more victims to satisfy his drive to eradicate anything that did not comply with Islamic laws, just like his plundering Arab ancestors. Having no time left, with the hurricane of events gathering momentum – wave upon wave of accusations followed by executions – I had to find, in a hurry, somewhere to live until this, hopefully, died down. I was lucky to locate a tiny attic room under the tin roof of an obscure little house in downtown Tehran, whose owner was a close friend of my father.

As often happens when one has to live in a temporary place, at first I thought I would only stay there for a short while until my friends could find somewhere a bit larger and habitable. From the first my life became a nightmare, worsening by the day as the horrors going on in the outside world started. I was totally cut off, twenty-four hours a day, from the life going on out there. I had to read and write by the gleam of a candle. In order not to raise any suspicion among the neighbours, who were always poking their noses into other people's -affairs, I was not allowed to have a small radio or television. The curtain was drawn and the straw blinds outside the window were down day and night.

Every day, just before break of dawn, the old lady of the house, whom I had always called Naneh Tabrizi since my childhood, would make a silent visit to my cubbyhole. She would then ask me to climb down the dimly-lit stairs to carry my breakfast tray back up to the tiny room. I would place the tray of tea things, *sangak* bread and a lump of cheese on the floor and begin to eat quietly. She would then leave as softly as a mouse to look after her invalid husband. As she closed the door behind her I could hear her muttering curses against the Imam and all his ancestors who had brought so much misery to our land. Feeling sorry for me, when she brought up my meagre supper late in the evening, she would stay on a bit longer and chat in the feeble light of the candle. During those quiet hours of the night, when the inhabitants of Tehran were fast asleep, dreaming their dreams populated with demons and ghouls, the old lady and I remained awake by telling stories to one another in that tiny, dimly-lit attic. She would start her stories with those she had told me a very long time ago during my childhood whenever she stayed with us. Her kind, trembling voice transported me once again to those far-off places and times – times of heroism and hope – when great men and women fought hard to make Iran a better place for all.

During those distant days of my childhood, now almost lost in the mists of time, at the start of every summer, I would, every day, climb up to the roof of our house with my textbooks and a small *kilim* tucked under my arm, sit in the shade of the *kharposhteh*, and revise my lessons. Just after noon, when the neighbours were having their afternoon nap and the area slumbered, Naneh Tabrizi would come up on to the roof and sit beside me as quiet as a little girl who wants to know what her older brother is up to on the roof all day. She would then scan the roofs that shimmered in the blazing sun. From time to time I would throw secret glances at her wise profile that I loved so much to look at. Every now and then she would heave a sigh, gently pulling her snow-white headscarf down to her brow. At moments like this I would forget all about my revising and the upcoming exams as the sleepy chirping of the sparrows that hopped about the rooftops sent me to the land of reveries, adding to the pleasure of those unforgettable moments. She would, all of a sudden, come to life and without casting a single glance at me, start relating stories of her childhood. As she told her stories, she nodded, every now and then, towards some old buildings or districts in and around which so many heroic deeds happened during those glorious days of the Constitutional Revolution. To the ears of the child that I was all these tales about those great men and women sounded very exciting. Only later on in my life did I come to understand the immense significance of those epic times for our nation.

One evening when she came up to my attic she looked unusually agitated and thoughtful.

"You look a bit troubled, *Naneh*?" I asked, as I puffed away at my cigarette.

"I'm getting more and more worried about you, dear." She sighed one of her painful sighs.

"Why? I think I'm safe here."

"I know, but those born-out-of-wedlock bastards have started sniffing around the neighbourhood, That worries me a lot."

"I don't think they can suspect a peaceful old couple like you of sheltering someone."

"You have no idea what sort of murderers these misbegotten mollahs are like when you go against them."

"I'm sure you know more about these bastards than I do."

"A lot, dear, a lot," she said. Dark thoughts cast their shadows on her wizened face. She waved her hand as if shooing away a swarm of gadflies and asked, "Why is it that so many miseries keep crashing on top of our heads?"

"You see, Naneh," I began to explain, "this is what I think. Some of the causes of the catastrophes we're suffering from now spring from fairly recent times. Since the shameful Anglo-American *coup d'état* of the nineteenth of August 1953 that put an end to Dr Mosaddegh's democratically-elected government and brought the Shah back to power, the people have been feeling deeply insulted and humiliated. The regime of the Shah didn't give a damn about their human dignity."

"You're right, dear." She nodded.

"But the real roots of our problems run very deep in our dark history," I went on. "For centuries, blows raining from all directions on their heads have stunned these people. Not knowing where the next blow would come from, they have had to resort to extravagant myths and the many superstitions brought to them as souvenirs by a host of barbaric invaders. All of these archaic beliefs and customs have come down to us, in the course of the centuries, from past generations without us ever questioning them. These beliefs were brought to us in the dark ages by countless foreign invaders and settlers such as Babylonians, Assyrians, Chaldeans, Greeks, Romans, Jews, Arabs, Turks and Mongols.

"The Chaldeans and Assyrians were the source of magic and superstitions with their bloodthirsty gods, sacrifices, auspiciousness or inauspiciousness of hours or days and the influence of malevolent stars on the destiny of human beings. The Greek invaders brought their fortune tellers, little and large vengeful gods, demigods and goddesses, who had nothing better to do than fiddle with human affairs, siding with this king, revenging that prince or raping a pretty princess they were infatuated with. The constant wars with the Roman Empire made the Persians familiar with a bunch of rogue astronomers, charlatan dream-interpreters and opportunist astrologists.

"The Jewish immigrants, who long ago were invited by Cyrus the Great to settle in Persia, brought with them as gifts the age-old wizardry from the Egyptian and Saudi Arabian deserts. Finally, the invasion of Arabs crowned this monumental misery in Persia. The Jewish people, being blood relatives of the Arabs and of the same race, took the opportunity to spread these barbaric practices. Troops of Jewish and Arab *hadith*-writers, chroniclers, and a bunch of superstition-manufacturers joined them in propagating mountains of meaningless absurdities in the minds of hard-working, tolerably rational Persian folk. Before all these invasions, the good old Persians went about their daily lives, working hard to create and maintain one of the oldest civilisations on this planet and minding their own business. They were happy people and took great pride in enjoying what life offered them in this world, leaving the other one to fantasists and a load of good-for-nothing idlers who lived off the toils of poor peasants and labourers.

"The invasion of the Arabs not only confirmed the earlier superstitions, but also added a completely new

118

range to them. Among the infinite number of absurdities one can only count but a few – the doctrine of one God who created Satan to tempt Adam and Eve in the Garden of Eden, the Fall from Heaven, life after death, Hell, Purgatory, Paradise, Doomsday, the idea that this world is just a passage leading to another one in which one can live forever with *houris* and *ghelmans*, the predominance of death over life, the superiority of torment over joy of life, the profanity of the human body, the existence of all manner of winged angels and wingless jinnis, the influence of fate in human affairs, leaving things to destiny, Sharia Law, fasting, unending prayers, prophecy, countless miracles attributed to Islamic saints, the dominance of men over women, being able to have many wives and an infinite number of *sieghehs*. These laws and rules have been infecting our lives from cradle to grave. All in all, they were too much for ordinary Persians to cope with.

"When the Persians rebelled against the Arabs in order to get rid of them and their irrational faith, they were crushed so mercilessly that they could never even dream of asserting their own customs and traditions again. The defeat was so severe, so absolute and painful that they ended up being even more fatalistic than ever. In the course of the centuries, these primitive beliefs have paralysed their mental faculties. They try to explain everything by falling back upon superstitious balderdash."

I paused and lit up another cigarette. Naneh Tabrizi sat there, thinking, no doubt, about what I had said.

"Add to this stinking cesspool of religion and ignorance, the frightening lack of real enlightenment that we never had, as happened in Europe after the Renaissance," I continued.

"I have a vague idea as to what it means," Naneh said, "but can you tell me more about it, dear?"

"My understanding is this, Naneh. It's a period in European history characterised by humanist thinking. It means that many enlightened people began to explain things, not by referring to God or religion, but by scientific experiments. Characteristics of the Renaissance are usually considered to include intensified classical scholarship, scientific and geographical discovery, a sense of individual human potential, and the assertion of the active and secular over the religious and contemplative life. And above all, in my view, was the rediscovery of laughter."

"Laughter?" Naneh Tabrizi repeated, baffled.

"Yes, Naneh. Laughter. For the first time great writers began to make a mockery of all those corrupt, pompous, serious-looking religious scholars and popes who thought they knew everything and could explain all the phenomena by referring to sacred texts."

"I like that, dear," she agreed, giggling mischievously. "If that's what you mean by Renaissance, it all started to happen during our Constitutional Revolution. My father, who took part in the Constitutional Revolution in Tabriz, read to me many pieces written by those poets and writers who made fun of mollahs. They made me laugh so much when I was a young girl."

"That's right, Naneh. Many of those pieces have also made me laugh a lot. As to the Constitutional Revolution being the start of a Renaissance in our land, I couldn't agree more with you. As always happens in our history, it all ended up in total failure and disaster. Going back in time centuries ago, if ever anyone like Omar Khayyam, Zakariya Razi or Hafez were brave enough to criticise the established ways of thinking, he'd be threatened with assassination, silenced in some way, or endlessly persecuted. Many books written by these courageous men were burnt in public to teach other freethinkers a lesson. Our tortured history shows that when people are oppressed for long periods and are not allowed to think freely for themselves, they hark back to primitive ways of behaviour, bringing back to life the ghosts of ancient superstitions and supernatural powers to seek explanations for events. After his expulsion by the Shah, Ayatollah Khomeini was turned, overnight, into a saintly hero. He remained the only real hope of opposing the Shah's regime."

"I remember even many big-headed scholars thought of him as a holy man and pinned their hopes on him," Naneh said.

"He had not even arrived in Iran before he was turned into a saint whose image appeared on the moon," I reminded her. "Do you remember how gangs of 'face-on-the-moon' vigilantes were roaming the streets of Tehran in those days, stopping ordinary folk everywhere, asking them if they had seen the image of the Ayatollah on the moon?"

"How can I forget those dark days?" she said, sighing.

Outside I could hear the distant, muffled sounds of the city of Tehran and wondered what horrors were being committed under the cover of darkness. It was far gone past midnight. I helped Naneh Tabrizi to stand up and wished her goodnight. She disappeared through the door into the shadowy landing.

*

Using various cunning ploys, a few of my trusted friends continued to visit me secretly at ungodly hours to see if I needed anything and to keep me informed of the latest horrors going on in the city. They told me that I was now in serious danger. I could not go anywhere till they found another solution. Meanwhile things got much worse and my stay in my secret hideout dragged on for several weeks. Throughout those weeks I did not keep quiet. Despite the risks, I persuaded my friends to publish a newspaper which was distributed secretly.

Fearful of our activities, the regime stepped up its suppressive tactics by contacting my wife and relatives, interrogating them non-stop about my whereabouts. They even took my old father to the Revolutionary Committee and cross-examined him several times. Not being able to get anything out of him, they insulted and slapped him and finally let him go. They then started to call my brother, who was a doctor in a large hospital in Tehran, and questioned him about me and whether he could help them to find me. My brother, of course, did not cooperate and was left in peace.

One evening, well after midnight, as I was sitting in the half-dark attic writing, my trustworthy contact walked in, followed by someone who looked like an apparition in the gloom. I raised my head from the paper, and recognised Jahaangir only when his pale face was lit up from below by the flame of the candle. His huge, dancing shadow, cast on the wall behind him by the flickering gleam of the candlelight, put me in mind of the devil himself. I jumped up and gave him a hug.

"I'm so happy to see an old friend," I said.

"Good to see that you're safe and sound, Behrouz," Jahaangir said, looking troubled. His now bearded gaunt face looked even more hideous at close range.

"Safe and sound, maybe," I said with a bitter smile, "but certainly not happy, cooped up like a convict, day in day out, in this cubbyhole, waiting for the angel of death to honour me with his visit one of these days."

"At least you're alive and still battling on," Jahaangir said, his haggard face cracking open with a smile.

Having heard terrifying news on a daily basis, I was filled with dread seeing Jahaangir's corpse-like face.

"Hmm, alive!" I muttered. "Do you call this living? For centuries all our writers and poets have done nothing but write about suppression, poverty, tyranny of all kinds, and have tried their damnedest to break the back of this fucking religion that has plagued our land for fourteen hundred years. At the time of the Pahlavi regime we were humiliated, imprisoned and tortured just because we were asking for the most basic rights for our people. When the revolution happened we, naively, became hopeful for a while that things might get better. Alas, the spring of freedom was short-lived and we were back to square one, yet again. After all that sacrifice and torment I've now ended up in this cubbyhole, hibernating like a wretched dormouse. You might say I'm active by writing these mind-numbing articles about mollahs and freedom of expression and all that crap to save the nation that has never given a hoot about our sacrifices. I want to write plays, short stories, and novels about ordinary people in which I celebrate life in all its glorious contradictions and complexities as the great European writers did without being hassled by those in power. I want to write about devils, about things to make people laugh and cry, and not be constantly reminding those motherfucker kings, mollahs, and imams about our natural human rights. After all those nightmare years at the time of the Pahlavis,

123

ninety-eight per cent of those imbeciles who inhabit this land voted for the Islamic Republic without even asking a single question about what it consisted of. You know what our nation reminds me of? Of those serial flunkers when we were in high-school, who never learned anything from their mistakes and when finally they left the education establishment, joined the hordes of those lumpen thugs who became the backbone of the uprising – the present day Hezbollahis and *Basijis* militia."

"I understand perfectly what you're saying, Behrouz," Jahaangir mumbled, gazing at the candle flames. Strangely, I noticed no conviction in his voice. I knew that he had something to say, but was hesitant about how and where to start.

"You shouldn't have come here, Jahaangir," I said. "If those bastards find out about your visit, we'll all be sent to hell, after being tortured to death, naturally."

"But I was the only one who could see you before it is too late."

"What do you mean, the only one?" I asked. "Why is it too late?"

"Yes, mate, too late."

"Why?"

"Because they've arrested everyone." The playful flame of the candle made his shadow dance on the wall, shapeshifting like a silently sniggering goblin.

"What do you mean by everyone?" I asked, staring him in the eyes.

"I mean all the writers, poets, actors whom we've known for years."

"But why?"

"I'm surprised a person like you is asking such a question. You of all people should know these murderers better than anyone else."

"I know, I know," I agreed. "Every day I feel as if someone clobbers me with a bludgeon, waking me up to the terrifying reality that our nation is undergoing these days."

"I've come to let you know it's in your best interests that the sooner you leave this place the better," Jahaangir said. "Everybody is now spying on everybody else. No one can be trusted these days. People are accusing others of treason and disloyalty to the Islamic Republic for trivial and imaginary reasons such as if they don't go often to a mosque or attend anti-American demonstrations. Mistrust is hanging in the air like the foul odour of miasma. Even family members cannot trust one another. Anyone can walk into a house, claim he's a government agent, and arrest whoever he fancies and hand them over to the Revolutionary Committees that are mushrooming in every district."

For fear of having been followed and thinking of my safety, Jahaangir had to leave with my friend. I sat down, brooding over his news. I tried to write, making my article as biting and poisonous as possible, but I felt swarms of vermin had invaded the inside of my skull, distracting me from the job in hand. I put the paper aside, blew the candle out, and tried to sleep. How can I sleep peacefully while most of my friends are in prison and the devil knows what is happening to them, I kept thinking.

It was just before daybreak that I fell into a shallow sleep, troubled by bad dreams. I heard a loud bang that sounded like the main door being opened and shut. Someone rushed into the courtyard. I could hear some hushed hustle and bustle in the room on the ground floor. Some people were speaking in subdued voices. Next I heard heavy footfalls on the stairs. I emerged from sleep, peered into the pitch dark and listened. The door of the attic room was quietly pushed open. When I recognised Naneh Tabrizi's form standing on the threshold I felt reassured, realising that I was fully awake and relieved that it was all just a bad dream. But as soon as Naneh Tabrizi stepped inside, she was followed by a figure veiled in a black chador. The faint light coming from downstairs cast her long shadow on the ceiling.

"Agha Behrouz, wake up," Naneh Tabrizi whispered, sounding panic-stricken and bending over me.

"I'm awake, Naneh," I mumbled.

"You've to leave this place as soon as you can."

"What? Have they come after me?"

"No, no, not yet."

"Who's that woman, then?"

"She's a very trusted friend of ours who lives a few houses down the lane," Naneh said. "I told her about you so that she can keep an eye on things as I cannot go out a lot. She's come to warn us that the mollahs' men are in the lane, searching all the houses for some young men whom they believe live in a safe house somewhere here. You must get away as soon as possible."

"What's the best way to get out?"

"You are to climb to the roof with my friend, and when the coast is clear, she'll take you down to her attic."

Hearing this, I was relieved. At first, seeing that black-chadored woman, I'd immediately though that I was done for. I thought she was definitely one of those Zainab

Sisters who had sniffed something suspicious in the house and had come to catch her prey.

I jumped up and put on my shoes, ready to go. Naneh told me not to worry about my papers, as she would get rid of them safely.

The black-veiled woman quietly led the way up the stairs to the *kharposhteh*. After scanning the nearby roofs, bathed in the milky-blue of the dawn, she signalled to me to follow her out. Crouching, we scuttled to the roof of her house and stepped into her *kharposhteh*, the door of which she locked from behind.

Having searched her house and not found the quarry they were after, the dogs of the regime did not bother to come back; they were busy searching too many other houses in the jungle that was Tehran. My stay in that *kharposhteh* lasted only one day. My friends who came to see me in the attic room were informed by Naneh Tabrizi of my last-minute flight. The same day, well after midnight, they came to take me away. One of them stood at the entrance of the lane to make sure that all was clear. Once satisfied, he gave a signal by lighting up a cigarette. The friend who had stayed with me beckoned to to step out into the lane and walk calmly to a car that was waiting for us. Once in the car, I stretched out on the back seat and the driver drove around the quiet streets till we arrived at a tumbledown building somewhere in midtown Tehran. After making sure no one suspicious was around, they told me to get out of the car and walk normally to the door of the building.

The friend, who had worked in that building in the past, pushed the door open and we stepped inside. Once the door was shut behind me I looked around and realised that it was an abandoned film studio that must have been ransacked by thugs during the uprising. We found our way to the main studio, in which, my friend told me later, many films had been made. How many popular actors and actresses, who are now out of work and have lost their livelihood, acted in those films, I wondered. The friend, who had himself acted in a few films made in that studio, suggested that I should hide behind the ramshackle scenery and broken-down props till morning. They promised me that they would return at night and take me somewhere else, hopefully a safer place. They handed me a sandwich, a packet of cigarettes and a lighter and left me alone in that godforsaken dark place. I lit a cigarette and took a much-needed drag to calm my ragged nerves, hiding its glow in the cup of my hand. I sat on the floor and began to mull over the events of the past year, my arrested friends, my wife who was not able to come and see me for fear of being followed, the future of my homeland, and a host of chaotic memories.

Exhausted from lack of sleep and all the excitement, I leaned my head against the wall. In a few seconds my eyelids became heavy and I fell into uneasy drowsiness. I could faintly hear the growling of that monstrous city, Tehran, stirring and stretching itself before waking up fully in order to devour, yet again, fresh victims for its rotten belly. As daylight began to find its way through the smashed window panes and rickety doors, I became wide awake. I stood up and gingerly found my way through the junk left from former times to explore the place a bit. I stepped through a gaping gash at the bottom of a large sheet of plywood that looked like the backdrop of some sort of scene. I had hardly slipped through the gash when I saw that it was indeed the wretched relic of an old stage put together to film a scene in a cabaret, the kind that featured in so many of those popular old films.

Many of those scenes, one by one, came to life on that pitiful stage in my imagination. I looked around and saw a small band of musicians, all wearing dark glasses, who sat, grim-faced, in front of the gaudily painted backdrop, strumming and scraping on their instruments, producing a mawkishly sentimental tune. An actress in a very short skirt wriggled her bum, showing her ample buttocks and singing some love ditties about the torments of unrequited love and the unfaithfulness of the beloved. I stood motionless on that desolate stage and saw in my mind's eye the audience made up of day-labourers, shopkeepers, gamblers, racketeers in fedoras, knife-fighters who were the henchmen of tough-necked strongmen and prostitutes, who drank, smoked, clicked their fingers, and danced on the tables. All of these people applauded the half-naked actress while ogling her plump legs and buxom breasts. Where were they now? What were they doing? How were they earning their living in that plague-ridden city? I couldn't help thinking of that poet-dancer-actress who ended up as a bag-lady. She must be sleeping rough somewhere in that barbarous city, alone and completely forgotten by her onetime admirers.

Late at night that day I heard some noises in the grounds of the studio. I hid behind the scenery, unsure who the intruders were. Once on the stage they whispered my name. I peered through the gash and made out the figures of my friends. They told me that as the cannibals of the regime were prowling everywhere, hunting hard for me, it was vital for me to change my appearance as much as possible. Being a wanted man, I had to do whatever they told me to do as they knew what was going on outside. One of them held the flame of a lighter in front of my face and the other produced a pair of scissors and began to cut my thick hair, just like the barber did years ago on my first day of military service. He then took out an electric shaver, muffled its noise with a handkerchief, and shaved the stubble on my head. Next, he sheared off my bushy moustache. As I had not the luxury of a mirror to look at myself, I could only imagine that shorn of my hair and moustache, I must look like one of those hairless devils in the underworld. To be completely on the safe side, they gave me different clothes. No one now would recognise me in my new get-up as I looked like a proper clown in one of those old films, I thought.

They drove me to a derelict caravanserai, used by water-carriers of olden times, which was located around an ancient water reservoir on the outskirts of Tehran near the brickworks, close to the shantytowns. Skinny mongrel dogs, stray cats, rats, and cockroaches lived alongside the addicted down-and-outs, creatures forgotten not only by the mollahs, but also by most of the people, and above all by Allah. Every day after dusk, these wretched men, like lost souls in purgatory, would shamble, singly or in twos, into the caravanserai. In rags and looking in desperate need of a fix, each would find a place around holes in the floor, choked with ash, in which they would prepare small fires using wood left from some junk or other. As despair and dire need can drive anyone to become inventive, they had made simple devices to smoke their opium. One of these gadgets was a bent metal wire shaped into a tong with which they took a glowing piece of ember, held it under a small sheet of aluminium foil, fished out from the garbage dumps in the surrounding vacant lots, on which was placed a morsel of impure opium. As the opium sizzled, they would hold the sheet under their nostrils and inhale the thick smoke. Once they were high, they would fall into such oblivion that they would forget what was going on around them. In the darkness, the glow of the burning embers cast a dim light from below on their wasted faces, making them look like demons squatting round a fire in a subterranean cave.

This nightly ritual of smoking opium would go on till they would slump, one after the other, into a deathlike torpor from which nothing in this world could rouse them. One would sit with his head drooped on his chest, another with his head propped on his knees, and the rest would stretch out around the fires, like soldiers after a lost battle. My worst nightmare began when the fire slowly went out and we were all covered under the black *abaa* of darkness. Instead of the cheerful chanting of water-carriers of bygone years, the place was filled with the ghastly symphony of snoring, groaning, and grunting of the addicts in their death-like sleep. Go on sleeping, my brothers; maybe you're right to choose the land of oblivion over this plague-infected land of ours, I thought. All this, combined with the foul stench of unwashed bodies, the devil knows for how long, drove me to the point of losing what little sanity I was left with.

One late evening they invited me to join in their opium-smoking ceremony. Not wishing to be considered an outsider to their community of brotherhood or hurt their feelings, I accepted. That was the first and last time in my life I smoked opium. Only then did I realise why those poor souls were doing it. For a few hours I forgot all my sorrows and felt a kind of ecstasy at being with these outcasts whom the world had abandoned. In my opium-induced drowsiness, I heard a heavenly tune played on a violin to which I shook my head like a dervish overcome by mystical ecstasy. As the sound became louder and louder I made out, bleary-eyed, someone playing a violin. He was a tall, grim-looking man in shabby clothes, sawing with all his might on the strings of his clapped-out instrument. With every flourish he wriggled his bum, croaking a street song with feeling. Hearing this, some of the addicts slowly came to life and started to clap feebly, keeping time with the music in their sleepy voices. One of them all at once sprang to his feet and began to dance, accompanying the rhythms. I had heard the song before in a popular play in a theatre in Lalezaar long ago.

You drove a hundred secret arrows into my heart,
Yet you ask me why my skin has turned as yellow as turmeric.
You, who knows all about me, why feign ignorance?

Once this wretched merriment stopped, they croaked eternal friendship to one another and lapsed again into their own different worlds, dozing and mumbling disjointed phrases to themselves.

My friends, realising that I couldn't go on like this, found another place in the basement of an old lodging-house with only an old man as a tenant. *Mash* Rajab, whom one of my father's friends knew quite well, was known to be the staunch enemy of anything to do with Islam. His forefathers were born and lived in Tehran, the city that, for centuries, had been a hotbed of untold treacheries and vices, begot by the hypocritical Islamic clerics, incompetent Ghajar kings, and countless foreign spies. As a consequence, he was a Tehrani through and through, an inveterate *arrack* drinker who lived a full life of pleasure during the reign of the Shah, spending most of his evenings with his like-minded mates in drinking taverns in Lalezaar or with prostitutes in *Shahr-e No*. Being the descendant of tolerably intelligent and cultured forebears, he was endowed with a bit of a philosophical streak, learning from his vast repertoire of experiences. Some nights, well after midnight, gripping a bottle of home-made *arrack*, he would totter down the dark staircase to keep me company. In the gleam of the candlelight, as we drank straight from the bottle, he chatted about his hero, the King of Kings and the Sun of the Aryan Race. How the Shah, following in the steps of his great, crowned father, dragged Iran out of the dark ages by pushing ahead with his modernisation programmes. The old man particularly admired Reza Khan the Cossack for his brutal stand against lazy people and the reactionary forces. As he was drunk and I was not in a mood for any argument about the nasty side of both kings, I just listened to him, nodding my agreement as I saw no point in disagreeing with this jolly, no-nonsense old man who had become so hardened in his ways and views, and who reminisced non-stop about his simple pleasures when a young man. Besides, I had to remain in his good books and must not make an enemy of him as my life was in his hands.

One night, over the *arrack* bottle, as we were discussing the frightening direction the revolution had taken, I decided to find out Mash Rajab's views on Iranians.

"Mash Rajab," I asked him, "being a man of the world who has seen and done so much in your life, why do you think this is happening to us?"

"You see Agha Behrouz," he said tipsily, "our problems are plentiful."

"I know, Mash Rajab, I know," I agreed. "I wonder if you could pick out a few of them so that I may learn a thing or two from you."

"I can only think of the three most important ones," he said before falling into deep thought.

"What's the first one, then, Mash Rajab?" I had to prod him as he had kept quiet for too long.

"The first one is that we act like conceited fools," he said.

"That's absolutely true, Mash Rajab," I hastened to agree. He sank into another brooding silence.

"And the second one, in your view?"

"What?" he said, as if waking up from a dream.

"The second problem that we have."

"Oh, yes, right you are, the second problem. It's the fact that we're vainglorious imbeciles who fancy we're superior to other nations."

"You hit the nail on the head, Mash Rajab."

It was now getting late and there was no sign of the third problem coming as Mash Rajab was now quite drunk and dozing off.

"Mash Rajab, Mash Rajab," I said, touching him gently on the shoulder.

"What is it?" He started awake and looked at me with bleary eyes.

"Let's finish off our conversation with you telling me about the third foible that we're afflicted with."

"Foible?" he repeated, evidently not knowing what I was referring to.

"The foibles of our nation you were just talking about a minute ago," I repeated, trying to keep my voice down.

"What a foolish nation, Agha Behrouz," he spluttered, gazing at the flickering candle-flame.

134

"Foolish indeed," I acknowledged. "What about the third shortcoming you promised to tell me?"

"*Ey baba*, Agha Behrouz," he said, fed up with my pressing him. "What's the use? There're too many of them and I'm stuck as to which one to choose."

"Anything that you're happy with."

"I know, I know," he said hazily. "Here's a nice one; the fact that we're self-seeking bastards."

Mash Rajab's head slowly dropped on his chest. I looked at this ordinary old man whom life had turned into a philosopher without his ever attending any school.

A few weeks were not out when I had to decamp. One day, before dawn, my friends came and hustled me away to a supposedly safer place – a remote location that only the devil knew where it was. This vagrant life of moving from one hideout to another was beginning to take its toll on my health when a friend found a clever solution.

Without our knowledge, fate, destiny, the malicious puppeteer who pulls the strings of we Iranians, or whatever you like to call it, is always up to his tricks, sorting out things for us, some auspicious, some inauspicious, some even outright hilarious. This time round I found its mischievous playfulness unexpected and positively amusing.

Well, the new hiding place that my friend found for me was the abandoned tailor's workshop in which we had rehearsed *Othello* nearly two months before, which exactly faced the United States Embassy. More than a year had gone by since the siege of the embassy and the taking of the hostages by a bunch of devotees of the Imam Khomeini. I thought the location would be a perfect place to witness one of the most ludicrous political shows in our glorious history. As the hostage crisis was in full swing at all hours of day and night, this would probably be the ideal way to put an end to my farcical life, the life of one living in the futile hope of bringing about a bit of positive change, however minuscule, to this benighted nation.

The safest time to go to the workshop was at midday, when the street in front of the American Embassy was choked with the demonstrating rabble. The stool pigeons of the regime, the Zainab Sisters, the Revolutionary Guards, and the Basijis, were far too preoccupied with trying to catch any foreign-looking spies mingling among the crowd to have enough time and resources to recognise me in my disguise among that motley multitude, who never stopped shrieking their heads off. When we desperately hunt for someone, we tend to ignore places that are just under our nose.

The workshop had a back entrance that opened to a quieter street. Once the car stopped in front of the door we got out, behaving like curious folk who had come to join the crowd. After casting glances around, we stepped inside the block in which there were several other workshops, all deserted. The one we were looking for was on the third floor. The workshop was in near darkness as all the blinds were down with their slats closed. Once my eyes became used to the gloom, I gave the room a quick once-over. To my surprise, I made out a number of mannequins left there on one side of the room. A few large sewing machines had also been left on one of the benches. I was told not to pull, never ever, the blinds up or switch on a light or smoke a cigarette. Any of these could raise suspicion. One should never, not even for an instant, lose sight of the fact that those whoresons, the ayatollahs and their henchmen, resemble that mythological monster, Argos, which had eyes all over its body so that when some of them were closed during sleep, the others remained wide open to keep watch for his countless imaginary enemies.

No sooner had my friends left the workshop than I stood up and walked to the mannequins and began to touch and smell them. They smelt of musty old chalk. As I traced my hand round their curves the flaking paint fell off their cold skins. I felt as if their lustreless eyes were winking at me meaningfully. Weary, I sat on a rickety chair and numbly contemplated my life. Being in a feverish state of mind, I felt that the mannequins, some standing on their flimsy props, some sprawling on the floor, others lying on their sides on the workbenches, were all watching me, and pointing at me, while whispering among themselves, like lepers who have just seen a newcomer in their colony.

As I mused over my strange life during the past months it became increasingly clear that, the way things were going, I was heading towards the abyss where the angel of death was waiting for me. The hyenas of the regime were shrieking louder and louder, calling other members of the pack to be ready for yet another feast. As the possibility of finding safer places was becoming slimmer, maybe this workshop was going to be the last port of call in my singular odyssey through Tehran. That colossal man of epic times, the renowned Odysseus, had so many cunning tricks up his sleeve which he used to escape from the misfortunes thrown ceaselessly in his path by malicious gods. Only one god, Allah, was against me – that vicious, vengeful god of Arab Muslims who had appointed a bunch of henchmen to hunt down people like me who just wanted to lead a free and happy life in our own homeland. My monsters were not the freakish creatures of myth, but men in turbans and *abaa* who had taken it upon themselves to carry out the laws concocted by that Allah who sat on his throne in heaven, surrounding himself with gorgeous angels, virgin *houris*, and pretty beardless *ghelmans*. Like an old tyrant whose reign is in imminent peril, this Allah stupidly demanded that his creatures worship him five times a day to keep them constantly on a leash. In order to sacrifice his thirst for blood, he ordered his freakish henchmen on earth to hunt me mercilessly with only one object in mind: to annihilate those like me from my people's memory.

In the land laid waste by Islamic ideology, men like me are transformed into impoverished fools whose clownish ruses are nothing but pathetic gimmicks that fail to work against that deep-rooted monstrosity. After ten years of wandering wine-dark seas, Odysseus returned to his home, Ithaca. For ten years he and his Achaean mercenaries had wreaked carnage upon the sacred city of Troy to save a beautiful woman, Helen, who had betrayed her husband and run off with a handsome Trojan prince. That epic character was a king with a beautiful wife, a young son, and even a faithful dog who never forgot him during the ten years of his absence. Full of hope, Odysseus was returning to all of them, who kept waiting for him to come back and put to the sword the persistent suitors who idled around in his palace, devouring all his goods and courting his queen.

"Who am I in this world?" I addressed the mannequins. "What is my role in the great scheme of things? Am I not just an insignificant little nobody who never had any claims to heroism whatsoever, let alone on an epic scale? Odysseus once told a lie to one of those one-eyed Cyclopes, claiming that he was called 'nobody' in order not to be eaten alive by the monster. Whereas I was born a nobody in this cesspool of a country and I will die a nobody, too. How could I claim to be somebody if the names and legacies of the greatest men and women born who fought for human dignity, freedom of thought and the right to live a joyful life in this land, were being systematically wiped from the face of our history? If these colossal figures are one by one driven into oblivion, who am I to be remembered? Sooner or later they will track me down, execute me without trial in one of those fucking Islamic Courts, throw my body in a garbage truck and carry me, in the dead of night, to an isolated spot in the hills on the outskirts of Tehran and dump it in a shallow grave, burying all the tell-tale signs. Knowing what Iranians are like, I will linger in the memory of a few relatives and friends and, once they are gone, too, I will join the lost battalion of phantoms who roam in the darkest depths of nothingness.

"Come to think of it, it is true to say that Odysseus and I fought, each after our own fashion, long-lasting battles. His was nothing but pillaging the magnificent city of Troy, taking young women captive and sharing them among his band of greedy soldiers, using all manner of tricks and treachery. What were my battles for, hey? They consisted of perpetual tiring skirmishes against the ignorance and stupidity of my nation, which, after betraying its own heroes, accepted and followed an invading Arab doctrine that destroyed its chance of becoming a great nation. That Odysseus fellow, after being tossed about on stormy seas, finally arrived at his homeland to be reunited with his wife and old friends, and live a happy life, in peace with his neighbouring states. Where am I now? What have I achieved, I ask you? After years of intellectual and artistic endeavours, doing my best to lead a civilized life, I have been rewarded with nothing but humiliation, imprisonment, and torture during both the Pahlavi era and the regime of mollahs, I am now a fugitive in my own homeland, fleeing like a frightened mouse from one hole to another to save my useless skin.

"After all those hard years of teaching, writing, directing, I am back to square one, sitting here, waiting to be caught like a quivering filthy rat and be chucked into one of those slimy ditches that run through the straggling shantytowns. I have gained no booty or pretty women from my battles, just lacerated knuckles from punching, over and over, at this gigantic wall of imbecility.

"In this, I would say to you, I resemble more that poor old man of myth, the absurd hero Sisyphus, who was condemned by the Olympian gods to live in the House of Death in the underworld. His punishment was to carry on his scrawny shoulders a monstrous boulder to the top of a mountain and place it there, only for the rock to topple repeatedly to the bottom of the mountain. Sweat drenching his body, dust swirling above his head, the wretched man kept humping the stone to the summit only for it to roll down time and again. You may ask why he was condemned to perform this futile task for eternity. I tell you why. His only crime was his scorn for the gods, his hatred of death, and his passion for life. All this won him that unspeakable penalty in which the whole being is exerted towards accomplishing *nothing*. This is the price that must be paid for the passions of this earth. Was I not paying dearly for my love of life in this skyless, oppressed country populated by traitors and fools, and ruled by tyrants? I was just an ordinary man who wanted to be happy and share some of his joys with his fellow countrymen, as a child does when he wants to share a new toy with his playmates so that they can enjoy them together."

An ear-splitting din coming from the street jolted me out of the delirious conversation I was holding with my patiently listening, mute audience. I peered into the darkness of the workshop, then stood up and groped my way to the window. Very cautiously, I opened a small gap between two slats of the blind and peeped to see what was going on outside. What I saw both shocked and amused me beyond words.

A horrific scene, bringing to mind the darkest days of my childhood in my native village that was home, more than anywhere else in Iran, to devilish Islamic rituals, was being played out in front of the American Embassy. A procession of heavily-bearded men draped in shrouds with their heads shorn bald was moving in two rows that faced each other. An apish-looking man was walking between the rows, braying a refrain into a loudspeaker in praise of Imam Khomeini. Behind him walked a young man who held aloft enormous brass cymbals, clanging them together like a village idiot, creating a racket. The men chanted and kept time with the rhythmic clashing of the cymbals by lashing their backs with sharp bundles of small chains, the handles of which they clutched. The blood from their lacerated flesh oozed out, making dark-red patches on the shrouds that glistened sickly in the gleam of the pale streetlamps. A pack of rough-looking thugs, hugging their Kalashnikovs, was prowling in front of the Embassy, not letting anyone near the massive wrought-iron gate, the two halves of which were chained together with chunky locks. A handful of other Kalashnikov-hugging neophyte neanderthals were perched on top of the tall wall of the embassy, acting as sentinels keeping watch over the vast, sprawling compound in which for so many years countless number of atrocities were planned and executed by the Americans in order to plunder my country. A haggard-looking, sleep-deprived crowd of women veiled in black chadors was standing a few metres away from the gate, screeching their own hackneyed slogans that I had been hearing over and over, day in, day out, after the revolution.

However freakish and entertaining the whole scene was, my eyelids became heavy and I decided to have some sleep. I groped my way over to the sprawling mannequin, grabbed it and placed it across the end of the workbench. Using it as a pillow, I rested my head on its cool belly. I closed my eyes, hoping to get a few hours of sleep, as I was by now completely knackered. No sooner had I fallen into a shallow sleep than a blast of cymbals, shrieking women, shots fired in the air, and other abnormal noises tore me from my slumbers. Even if I fell asleep for just a few minutes, my head was invaded by the roaring of hordes of barbarians brandishing clubs and yelling war-cries.

This waking nightmare went on till morning, when a pale daylight began to sneak in through tiny gaps in the slats in the blinds. Though groggy, I sat up with a start, and peered into the half-dark around me. For a moment I thought some people were standing in the corner of the room, silently watching me. The thought flashed through my mind that I was definitely done for. When they did not move, I realised that these apparitions were none other than my lifeless companions – the mannequins. Like unwanted statues kept in the basement of a ruined palace, they stood there in their different poses.

Hearing some muffled voices coming from the street below, I climbed down from the bench, tiptoed barefoot to the window, lifted one of the slats a crack, and peeped through the slit. Down in the street, in the milky-blue light just before daybreak, the usual crowd were bustling about, preparing for the same daily show ahead. Everybody was shuffling around in silence. The iron gate of the embassy was wide open. Under the sleepless, still watchful eyes of the Kalashnikov-hugging hostage-takers, cars carrying turbaned and *abaaed* men and vans carrying supplies were moving in and out of the embassy. A handful of thugs were busy diligently fixing banners on top of the embassy wall, while others were rushing here and there along the pavement, sticking even more posters on the already paper-choked wall.

The street vendors and hawkers had already started to set up their carts and stalls along the wide pavement that stretched along the whole of the embassy compound. The scene reminded me of the street markets at dawn outside *Shahr-e No*, where multitudes of uprooted peasants from the villages all over Iran had established their cheap and dodgy goods in the heyday of the renowned brothel. As the day progressed, droves of grim-faced and scruffy-looking street-traders flocked on to the pavement, the devil knows from what poverty-plagued parts of Tehran. As the newcomers pushed and shoved one another to find a spot in the rapidly crowding makeshift bazaar, scraps and brawls broke out.

The real casualties of these territorial disputes were the stalls and overloaded carts that were pushed out of the tight corners by the defending parties, making them trundle down the street with their loads tumbling in all directions. Fresh and half-rotten melons, watermelons, gherkins, salted walnuts in jars, an assortment of apples, half-rotten grapes, fresh and dried mulberries, shrivelled votive dates, sugar-coated roasted peanuts still in braziers, skewers of lamb-liver kebabs, plastic balls, small American flags, pictures of Imam Khomeini and Jimmy Carter, and all sorts of other goods littered the street. Seeing this shambles, a clutch of good-natured, middle-aged men interceded with the warring factions, reminding them, from what I gathered by the way they gesticulated, of the gravity of these events taking place in front of the 'Nest of Spies'. Upon listening to these wise men the traders had no choice but to shake hands and be more accommodating towards their fellow traders, otherwise they would be removed by the Revolutionary Guards who prowled everywhere to keep a semblance of peace.

Having seen the behaviour of my fellow countrymen on countless occasions such as wedding ceremonies, mosques, *tekiehs*, *ta'ziehs*, the festival of *Omar-koshaan*, during the festivities for the Coronation of the Shah, *Shahr-e No*, garden parties, overcrowded coaches travelling to and from my native village, countless holy shrines, drinking taverns, cabarets, gambling dens, opium haunts, and funerals in the graveyards, I had a good hunch that the day was going to be one of first-class entertainment not to be missed. As I had nothing else to do and could die any day soon, I thought I should make the most of it, relax and enjoy the most grotesque carnival ever performed in any country on this planet – the carnival of a confused nation which had completely lost the plot fourteen centuries ago after the Arab invasion. From the moment that our Persian civilisation was trampled upon by a bunch of barbarian Bedouins, nothing had been in its natural and proper place. Everything in our land had been dislocated in place and time, where anything, absolutely anything could go without anybody being able to understand why, nor even try to make sense of all this disorder.

I grabbed a chair, put it close to the window, sat down and began to watch the best comic show on earth. I felt the same excitement as when I watched the itinerant marionette show when I was a little boy, squatting with other boys and girls on the dusty ground in the village square.

By now the carnival of hate, folly, and lunacy was in full swing. This was a bizarre, home-grown carnival that had nothing to do with the joyfulness and unbridled revelling in the worldly pleasures of this life as happened in ancient times in many countries. The street below was swelling with a rabble, the dregs of Tehran, created and then abandoned by the Shah and his cronies before he fled to more exotic climes.

Different processions, made up of diverse crowds from all over Iran, appeared from one end of the street. Coming to a halt in front of the gate, they screamed their slogans and stampeded down the street, vanishing from view, no doubt to go back to their cheerless lives. The first comprised a huge mass of black-chadored, shrieking Zainab Sisters. They looked like a mass of black beetles that had emerged from subterranean caves. Each woman gripped the hem of her chador in one hand, holding aloft a small placard proclaiming 'Death to America.'

Following in their footsteps was a procession of bearded and stubbly old men, who shuffled slowly, many of them with the aid of sticks, rhythmically beating their chests and croaking as best they could the immensely popular slogan of 'Death to Israel.' No sooner had these elderly zealots passed the gate than a battalion of eager-looking, black-clad young men marched into the street.

They marched in two rows, facing one another, beating their chests with all their might in rhythm with the blare of trumpets and the clanging of cymbals. They came to a halt in front of the gate and there blasted into yelling the slogan, 'Khomeini fights, America frights.'

After these young men left the stage an army of workers from a variety of factories, as their banners suggested, appeared, crying "Bring back the Shah." What? Bring back the Shah! I was completely baffled. What did they mean by that? Under present circumstances it could definitely not mean bring him back to mount him on his throne, yet again! This time the man is gone for good, mates. If they meant to bring him back in order to kill him, it was definitely too late. He had fled with his millions of dollars stashed away, devil knows in what secret bank accounts somewhere on this planet, enough for him and his offspring to live a life of Croesus anywhere in this world. No power on earth could bring him back now, as some had been in the past. You fools, the highwayman, after raiding your caravan, has loaded his mules and fled to far-away mountains to enjoy his booty. Maybe the banner was a practical joke, or simply a stupid mistake committed in a hurry, as a lot of things are done in this land in such a rush, thinking only of the moment.

The last spectacle that appeared on the scene were rough-looking Basijis, carrying a gigantic, broadly smiling cardboard dummy of the American president, Jimmy Carter, with plump red lips. Looking like a scarecrow, it was garbed in an oversized jacket with stars and striped stitched on it. Once in front of the gate, they propped the scarecrow on the floor and began shouting, "Carter should be executed." They then danced around it, in the manner of primitive cannibals who dance around their victim, spitting and throwing all sorts of trash at it. After setting fire to it, they all jumped up and down on the charred remains of the President, yelling slogans. When they tired of that, they marched in small groups to the end of the street, looking pleased for having done their bit for the supreme leader whose colossal image, unsmiling and forbidding as always, hung on the wall beside the gate.

The motley pageant of other hoi-polloi, herded together from all over the land and rewarded generously by the mollahs, continued to pour into the street, playing their allocated roles. Job done, they rapidly melted into the swarm of uprooted peasants who lived a precarious existence, only called to service whenever they were needed. The permanently settled mob, however, stayed behind, encouraging the newcomers to join in that farcical imitation of a carnival.

By around midday the home and the world's media had established themselves behind the iron railings put up on both sides of the gate. The regime's own journalists were allowed into the compound to interview the hostage-takers to keep the propaganda machine going, whereas foreign journalists waited patiently in long queues along the pavements to be granted a glimpse of the inside of the compound. That happened extremely rarely. Small bands of eager cameramen and documentary makers, however, mingled among the rabble, filming away and asking questions.

All this commotion turned out to be very profitable for the hawkers and stall-holders, who did not give a toss what was going on around them. All they cared about in this chaos was to catch as many fish as possible from the muddy waters of everyday life – never-ending marches, meetings, gatherings, religious festivals and ceremonies, the commemoration of martyrs, Friday prayers, and a host of events that took place every single day. The hungry bellies of their wives and children would not comprehend the significance of hostage-taking, martyrdom, the warnings of the Koran about hell and its promises of eternal bliss in the other world, non-stop sermons in mosques about morality and how to be a model Muslim. Once the bellies of their families were full maybe they would show some sort of interest in religion and politics.

The street traders kept singing out their jingles, praising their goods, each in his own style, to sell as much as possible before these political shenanigans came to an abrupt end. So many changes in this land are short-lived and soon forgotten about. The moment you settle down to the new way of life some affliction falls from the sky on the heads of this cursed country and you have to accept the new realities and go along with the new order, otherwise you are branded as unpatriotic, a foreign spy, or a political dissident. Take advantage of any calamity that befalls you the best you can and be resourceful if you want to live a peaceful life, albeit for a short time, with a full belly. That is why the street traders had become as crafty as chameleons, only getting involved with all this political and religious lunacy when they could turn it into their own profits.

Overcome with curiosity to see this carnival of street traders at close quarters on such a unique occasion, I decided, like Odysseus who disguised himself as a beggar to spy on his wife and her suitors, to throw caution to the winds and join the crowd in the street. The henchmen of the regime, all being a bunch of imbeciles, would find it hard to spot me with my different appearance.

Once in the street, I mingled with the crowd, trying as far as possible to avoid the Revolutionary Guards. The traders carried on happily with their business, selling goods to different folk: American flags to frenzied demonstrators to burn or trample upon, Imam Khomeini's portraits to Zainab Sisters and Basijis, cheap rosaries to trainee mollahs who had been carted over from the holy cities of Qom and Mashhad, small copies of the Koran and all sorts of prayer books to the devout Muslims, cassettes of Imam Khomeini's speeches to keen students, lamb-liver kababs wrapped in *taftoon* bread to hungry young men who had come to flirt with the younger Zainab Sisters, plastic footballs and ready-to-fly kites to snotty little boys, candies to constantly howling little girls, sugar-roasted peanuts and salted walnuts to idle bystanders who had come there to enjoy the show for want of anything better to do.

Having lived an erratic existence from the day they stepped into this mean world, these traders had become adept at coping with all sorts of tricky circumstances. They sang the praises of their wares as they cast covert glances at the cameramen. As soon as a cameraman pointed his lens at one of them, the trader modified his pitch by inserting a suitable slogan into his song. If they were selling mulberries they would cry, "I have mulberries as sweet as honey. Death to Carter. Come on folk, sweet mulberries," without, in all likelihood, knowing who Jimmy Carter was. If they were selling lamb-liver kebab, they would sing, "Come and taste my tasty lamb-liver kebab with *taftoon* bread. Long live Imam Khomeini. Come on, tasty kebab." Once the cameraman turned his attention to another one, the trader would resume his normal chanting minus the slogan. Some traders, in order

149

to show their true loyalty to the Islamic Revolution and the person of the Imam, added an extra bit to impress the mollahs even more. They would shout, "Enjoy your kebab and don't forget to say 'Death to Israel' to secure your place in paradise in the next world."

Looking around to see no one was following me, I returned to the workshop around midday. This scandalous mishmash of a carnival, unique to Iranians, carried on every day from dawn to midnight, keeping me highly entertained. One day I asked one of my friends, who had come to check on me to see that everything was all right, to stay and watch the scene outside with me. After peeping through the slats, we sat a while on the workbench and talked about the tragi-comic behaviour of our people.

"I wish I could understand why these people change every event into such absurd shows of self-harming and hatred, Behrouz," he said in a low voice.

"If you ask me," I said, "I think we would have to go a very long way back in our history to find out the roots of most of these bizarre behaviours, Bahaador."

"I suppose you have a point," Bahaador agreed. "As you know, I'm an ordinary mathematics teacher turned cab-driver and don't know as much about our social history as you do. Where do you think we can find the roots?"

"At the dawn of our civilization," I said. "You see, Bahaador, during the Persian civilisation our forebears enjoyed popular festivals organized entirely by ordinary people. With the conquest by the Arab Muslims all these festivals were wiped out or, at most, were distorted by the ruling Islamic ideology. As a consequence, these festivals and merrymaking events lost their feeling of joyfulness and the celebration of life."

"How do you know these festivities happened?"

"We know about these pre-Islamic events mostly through the writings of the renowned Greek historian, Herodotus, who has described in his book *The Histories* an annual festival that he called 'Magaphonia', meaning the 'Killing of the Magus'. During this spectacle the street actors revealed, through a mixture of songs and miming, the crimes of the Magus who usurped the throne, pretending to be a king. At the end of the show the actors killed the mock king. While the show was going on, all the Magi hid in their houses and temples for fear of being attacked by angry spectators."

"This festival reminds me of the *Omar-koshaan* ceremony that I've heard of," Bahaador said.

"Spot on, Bahaador," I agreed. "This ancient spectacle could, most probably, be the origin of the later popular festivals with mock killings of kings and Islamic caliphs. This show was later on inspired by pre-Islamic mocking of Crassus festivals, *Kusseh-barnesheen*, and the *Omar-koshaan* of the Islamic period."

"So our ancestors were very much into merrymaking and enjoyed themselves?"

"That's right," I said. "Even during their countless military campaigns they danced and sang to keep their spirits up. According to the Greek historian Xenophon, who joined the Greek mercenary army of the Achaemenian prince Cyrus the Younger, ancient Iranians, who were always at war with their distant neighbours to plunder their wealth and riches, had a time-honoured custom of trailing behind their large armies troupes of entertainers and clowns to keep the soldiers amused when they camped at night in remote oases or hamlets. During these shows the entertainers cried slogans, mocking the unknown enemy while performing warlike Persian dances and brandishing their shields, accompanied by kettle drums and flutes. These stratagems were designed to embolden the disenchanted soldiers to fight, to kill, and to wreak havoc on the adversary in a most brutal way."

"Where then did they manage to perform all those festivals during peacetime?"

"As there were no amphitheatres, like the ones in Greece of that time, or show-houses in those days," I explained, "these popular shows took place in public squares and marketplaces where people gathered to trade their goods, conduct official ceremonies, and exchange news."

"I wonder if Iranians learnt anything from the Greeks during all those wars."

"During those devastating wars with their near and far neighbours, Iranians definitely learned about shows in other cultures," I told Bahaador. "For complex cultural reasons, however, such as suppression and the long-established harsh class system, Iranians were not at all successful in creating powerful dramas as the Greeks did. Although the top layers of Iranian society were aware of Greek drama, the bulk of the population were not allowed to perform similar plays in Iran. Therefore, they were more than happy to remain as spectators sooner than become producers, directors or professional actors."

"So what was that festival of *Kusseh-barnesheen* which you mentioned earlier?"

"The heyday of the *Kusseh-barnesheen* festival was at the time of the Achaemenes Dynasty. It occurred, each year, at the start of the month of *Azar* (December)," I explained. "A man with a sparse beard, garbed in shabby clothes, would perch on a donkey, holding in one hand a crow, and in the other a large fan. He would eat hot food, then fan himself frantically, pretending he was boiling hot. The merrymakers would rollick around the donkey, laughing, splashing him with water, chucking lumps of snow at him, as well as rotten melons, bread, gherkins and other fruit and vegetables. The donkey-rider would catch some and munch away, throwing handfuls of red clay which he kept in a bowl on the packsaddle at those spectators who had not chucked food and vegetables at him.

"After the Muslim invasion this popular festival survived in many remote villages and towns, keeping its original farcical character. With the tightening grip of the Islamic faith on all aspects of life in our land, this annual spectacle gradually underwent profound changes to suit the taste of the Islamic caliphs and their Iranian lackeys. It was around the fifth century of the Islamic calendar that the nature and timing of this show was changed and it was called *Mir-e Nowruzi* or *Paadeshah-e Nowruzi*. This festival, despite all the odds against it, managed to survive until half a century ago in some cities and towns. It still goes on in some remote villages and hamlets that have somehow escaped the present Islamic regime's clampdown on all joyful events."

"This is the first time I have heard about a festival called *Mir-e Nowruzi*."

"I'm not surprised, Bahaador," I said sadly. "Even during the Pahlavi era this ancient cultural event was suppressed in big cities and towns as it made fun of the King of Kings. Those flunkies who kept the regime of the

Shah going wouldn't dare even mention it in their controlled media."

"So, as its name suggests," Bahaador said, "it took place around *Nowruz*?"

"Correct," I said. "This festival took place throughout the whole of the *Nowruz* and lasted for thirteen days. During the festivities this *Mir-e Nowruzi*, who was a freakish-looking man, would proclaim himself king by putting a large crown on his head and dressing himself in glittering clothes. He would sit on a makeshift wooden throne, prepared by the local carpenter, and make the people laugh by acting like a tyrant king. Mimicking the king or the ruler, he would issue ridiculous decrees, such as the confiscation of rich people's properties or an arrest warrant of this or that wealthy man, an incompetent prince or a man of power. The troupe of entertainers would then mount this jester-king on a colourfully decorated stallion with someone holding a huge umbrellalike sunshade to protect him from the sun. A party of fierce-looking footmen, attendants and lackeys, flanking the horse, would run along bullying the mob of spectators with their bludgeons to let the king ride through the lanes and alleys. The mob, pretending to be his subjects, would stampede helter-skelter around the horse, laughing and mocking the false king. A small band of men would carry long sticks on top of which were stuck the skulls of cows, donkeys, and sheep that represented the heads of the enemies whom the king had vanquished."

"No wonder it was abolished by the Muslim caliphs and their Persian arse-kissers," Bahaador said with a grim chuckle.

"The only thing these whoreson Arabs and their Persian yes-men were afraid of was when folk made fun of them."

"I suppose they can't tolerate being mocked. Laughter was and still is the greatest enemy of Muslim rulers."

"You're right, mate," I agreed. "Laughter is the most powerful weapon one can use against these fucking tyrants. They can't handle its liberating force. Faced with a comedian who makes a mockery of their beliefs, faith, and behaviour, all their ridiculous shams would be exposed to the light of day for all to see. They only survive when they live under the pall of darkness that they've spread over themselves and their wretched subjects. They resemble nasty little creatures of night that do not have any idea what sunlight is. The harsh light of day and reality would blind them, making them crawl into the nearest possible crevice or a crack in a wall."

"So, as the name of the spectacle suggests, it only lasted throughout Nowruz?"

"That's right," I said. "These noisy festivities would come to an end on the thirteenth day of Nowruz. After the thirteenth day, the glorious reign of the mock king would be over. The clown would then come out of character and put his clothes in a large chest to be used at the following Nowruz. These entertainers ran in families and the skill was handed down from one generation to the next. Some vestiges of this festival still occur in the form of dancers with charcoal-blackened faces in some districts of large cities. This joyful festival was another example of ordinary people's revenge on the tyrants who ruled them."

We sat there in the dark for a moment or two, listening to the pandemonium outside.

"Have you seen the effigy of Jimmy Carter that the mob burns every other day in front of the embassy?" I asked.

"I saw it on the News," Bahaador said.

"Doesn't it remind one of the *Omar-koshaan* ceremonies in many of our villages and towns?"

"It does indeed."

"Even the origins of this one can be traced back to ancient Iran," I said. "A popular show played by the ordinary folk before Islam at the start of the month of *Dey* (January) was to make an effigy of a king, place it in a public square or marketplace, and pay him due respect for a short while. The people would then set fire to the effigy, and trample upon it. Ordinary people used this spectacle to show their pent-up anger, in a farcical fashion, with tyrannical kings and rulers."

"Maybe this ceremony was also quashed by the Muslim rulers."

"You're right to say that, Bahaador," I said. "This mock-heroic show somehow managed to survive for nearly four centuries despite the brutal oppression dealt to festivals like that by the Islamic caliphs and their Persian flunkies. Eventually the practice was completely stamped out by the ruthless clampdowns and the prosecution of popular artists. The self-proclaimed representatives of Allah on earth deemed this festival pagan, therefore anti-Islamic, and extremely harmful to the faith that by now sat all over Iran like an incubus, suffocating all its age-old traditions and customs."

"So, I suppose whatever was left of it turned into what we call now *Omar-koshaan*."

"Yes. As always happens in this land, this spectacle, like many others, never completely died out, but changed its form and turned into an Islamic one, the one which we now call *Omar-koshaan*. The hatred and bitterness felt by the people against all tyrants in the original festival was stage-managed by the imams and clerics and channelled against a long-ago Islamic caliph in a distant place who was believed to have usurped the Islamic caliphate of -Ali, the son-in-law of the Prophet."

"Those Arabs freshly converted to Islam even fought among themselves for absolute power over their Bedouin tribes and the nations they conquered," Bahaador reminded me.

"You can only imagine how they would treat Iranians with that kind of power given to them by that vicious Allah of theirs," I said. "Anyway, being a uniquely Shiite invention, this grotesque festival reached its highest point of popularity at the time of the Safavid Dynasty who made Shiism the state religion by converting all Iranians to it, using the most brutal means possible."

"No wonder it has lasted to this day."

"Once a fanatical belief and practice is planted in the depths of the collective consciousness of a nation," I said, "no power on earth can uproot it. That's why it still goes on all over Iran, particularly in backward villages and hamlets, encouraged even more by the mollahs."

"I've never had a chance to actually see this ceremony," Bahaador confessed.

"I had the misfortune of seeing it several times in my native village in the remote parts of Azerbaijan," I said. "Every year, on an appointed day, the illiterate villagers gathered in the main village square in an anarchic, riotous atmosphere of festivity. They would pile up a large heap of brambles and twigs on dried-up dung slabs. They would then prop, smack in the middle of the heap, a scarecrow-like dummy created by tying pieces of wood together with twigs. Its head was made of an upside-down pitcher, inside which was stuck a long stick that acted as the neck and the body. On the pitcher were glued eyebrows, eyes, nose, and a mouth fashioned out of coloured paper pulp. A filthy, brownish tangle of wool formed its hair, moustache and beard. He was comically crowned with a moth-eaten white turban in the old Arabic style worn by Islamic caliphs. The wooden frame of the scarecrow was draped with a long, frayed *abaa*. A pair of worn-out, Arabic-style sandals, dangling precariously over the twigs, was fixed to its feet. The scarecrow was meant to look like Omar, the second caliph of Islam after the death of Prophet Mohammad. The folk would caper round the scarecrow, each shrieking a different song, laughing loudly, and hurling rude comments at it."

I fell silent, remembering. The bedlam outside carried on undiminished.

"Now, that is the legacy that fourteen centuries of Islamic rule in our land has left for us." I nodded towards the window. "Iranians were known to other nations, particularly to the Greeks because of Alexander's conquests, as a people who enjoyed drinking wine and singing and dancing during the many festivals such as *Nowruz, Mehregaan, Sadeh, Khordadgaan, Bahmangaan, Tirgaan, Azargaan*, and *Yalda Night*. Each one of them marked an important event or characteristic of humanity – love, friendship, birth, fertility, the beginning of a new season, the end of dark winter days, and the longest night of the year. We were the first to make wine and create the concept of paradise that comes from the ancient Persian word *pardis*, meaning 'House of Song'. We warmed our souls by drinking wine with our friends and companions. Music and dance were part of our everyday lives. Our paradise was here on earth. The one in the other world was just a reflection of this earthly one only because we wanted it to last, to stay with us after our death. How can you create a paradise in heaven if you have not lived it here on earth? Our festivals were full of laughter and great fun, free from any kind of suppression."

I had to stop. A wave of emotion surged up in my chest, stifling me. I felt as if the loss of all that had been was crushing my soul. How desperately I needed a cigarette to calm my frayed nerves.

"What's left of all those festivals and *joie de vivre*, hey?" I carried on, hardly able to breathe. "If you ask me, I'd say, nothing; nothing whatsoever. Our festivals these days are just pale and ridiculous shadows of those old ones. They happened in the lanes, markets, and streets, not behind closed doors for fear of revenge by the keepers of Sharia Law."

"We still celebrate *Nowruz*, though," Bahaador reminded me timidly.

"You're right, mate. I nearly forgot about that," I said with a mocking laugh. "Do you honestly call that a celebration of *Nowruz*? What we celebrate these days is nothing but a wretched, empty husk of one of the greatest festivals in all civilisations. Why should we have a copy of the Koran written in Arabic, in our *Haft Sin* arrangement for the *Nowruz*? Why should we welcome the start of our *Nowruz* by reciting some stupid verses in Arabic that no one comprehends? Why should we see the repulsive picture of the Imam Khomeini on television at the start of the *Nowruz*? To add insult to our countless injuries, instead of listening to music, to poems about the coming of the spring, and watching beautiful women dancing, we have to listen to the Imam and his turbaned and baboonlike cronies who talk endlessly about the eternal beauty of Islam and how fortunate we are to live in an Islamic country."

"All that is true," Bahaador agreed. "In fact I feel more depressed than ever during *Nowruz* instead of feeling cheerful."

"All we're left with now are the gruesome shadows of those once happy festivities," I said. "The Islamic ideology, after annihilating them, remade them after its own image – the incarnations of misery, mourning, hatred of infidels, love of death, and hatred of worldly pleasures; the banning of wine, music, dance, painting, sculpture – in a word, banning living altogether! One of their festivals happens after a month of the self-torture of fasting, during which you live almost like a dead man, giving up all worldly pleasures. Eid then follows, with the slaughter of sheep and gluttony. Another of their freakish festivals is when they commemorate the Prophet Abraham's willingness to sacrifice his son to that bloodthirsty Allah. Yet again, they cut the throats of flocks of sheep on the pavements and in the squares, making the cities filthy with blood and disembowelled guts, turning them into a vast slaughterhouse, as their ancestors turned the great cities of our land into abattoirs centuries ago."

I took a breather to gather my thoughts.

"As if all that was not enough," I went on, "the home-grown Shiite sect of Islam brought even more calamities upon this cursed nation by cooking up stories of the martyrdom of Imam Hossein and his clan in Karbala. During the month of *Moharram* our cities turn into vast graveyards in which funeral processions for an Arab man take place. Millions of Iranians all of a sudden go berserk by beating their chests, flagellating themselves with razor-sharp iron chains, shrieking and wailing for an Arab man whose barbarous tribes invaded our land and laid it waste in the name of a new religion the devil only knows where it sprang from."

The noises outside had grown to a loud rumble.

"Instead of the hearty laughter that rang in the squares and market places in ancient times we now hear nothing but the guttural braying of the Koran readers, muezzins calling for prayer in every bleeding mosque all over the city, the rhythmic, nauseating thuds of chest-beating, the stomach-churning jangling of self-flagellation, the screeching of ravenlike, black-veiled hags, ugly Zainab Sisters wrapped in black chadors, the eternal bellowing of mollahs in mosques and on radio and television, and endless marches and demonstrations against America and Israel."

It was getting late.

"Things don't look good, Behrouz," Bahaador said.

"No, not good at all," I agreed, thoughtful now that I had got so much of what angered me off my chest .

"I'll have to leave you again." Bahaador was apologetic. "Hopefully, I'll see you soon and let you know about the latest developments."

We shook hands and he left. As the shutting of the entrance door rang in the deserted block I wondered whether I would see him again. One could never tell in those days of the reign of terror.

A few days later, at daybreak, Bahaador walked into the workshop. Whenever someone walked in like that I would say to myself, "That's it, they've come to get me."

"Bad news, Behrouz," he said, his voice trembling. "This time things are very serious."

"What do you mean by serious?" I asked. "Have they found out where I'm hiding?"

"Not yet," Bahaador said. "But we have to leave this place quickly."

"Where are we going now?"

"Truth be told," Bahaador replied cautiously, "out of this country this time."

"What?" I nearly shouted, not believing what I heard. "What do you mean out of this country?"

"That's exactly what I said," he said. "It's now impossible to hide you anywhere here in Tehran. All the houses, vacant plots, ruins, and every nook and cranny of this city are now suspicious places to the bearded dogs of the regime. They've stepped up arresting people for the slightest of excuses and executing the dissidents, no matter who they are. A lot of people such as artists, writers, poets, as well as both rich and ordinary people have already fled, leaving everything behind and using any means available to them."

"How can I leave my homeland?" I protested. "Despite all the horrors and the madness that goes on here, I still love this land. My roots of thousands of years are far too deep to be yanked out and planted in foreign soil. Before you could even plant me there I'd wither and die. Even if I lived a while, I'd soon wilt away as the customs, history, traditions, and the language of that foreign land are not mine. If I cannot write in my own language, I'll be of no use to anyone."

I stopped and regarded Bahaador's profile in the gloom.

"What's more," I went on, "how about my wife, my father and mother, my brother and sisters, my friends, the greengrocers, the bakers, the cab drivers, the street pedlars and hawkers in the lanes and in the market places who sing so beautifully the praises of their goods? How about those, hey? How about the lanes and alleyways that come alive with women and children on hot summer evenings? How about the kids who run in the gutters looking for rusty coins? How about the ragamuffins who play with deflated plastic balls in every lane and vacant lots? How about the blossom-laden apple, apricot, and cherry trees at the start of the month of *Farvardin*, heralding the coming of *Nowruz*? How about the kids who, dressed up in their once-a-year new clothes during the *Nowruz* festivities, parade in the alleyways and pavements, showing off to their friends? How about the young men, garbed in cheap suits of the latest fashion, who strut around like young cockerels on the street corners with cigarettes between their lips, casting amorous glances at the young ladies dressed in tight trousers and short skirts? How about the sparrows trilling on the roofs and walls? How about the flocks of crows that invade the rooftops to welcome autumn with their melancholy cawing? How about those purple-hued mountains that slumber like old hermits wrapped in their rags on the north of Tehran? How about snow-capped Mount Damaavand that looks like the dome of our land and stands like a worn-out but proud sentry outside the city, hiding dark secrets of untold treacheries and crimes in its volcanic belly?"

Bahaador was staring at me.

"You know what, Bahaador?"

"What?" he muttered.

"Mount Damaavand and the Alborz Mountains Range whisper to me. They tell me countless tales of so many treacheries, back-stabbings, betrayals of our best men and women. They tell of untold cruelty committed for centuries by our people on their countrymen in this whorehouse of Tehran. Only these mountains know what happened, since so many books and documents were burnt and destroyed by the Arabs, Moguls and countless other invaders, assisted by their Persian lackeys."

"You're speaking the truth, Behrouz," Bahaador said when I paused for breath, "but things are changing with shocking rapidity. Like lunatics who have at last found their chance to rule, these mollahs are jumping up and down, trampling on all that we've held dear for centuries. Our ancient customs, our age-old ways of living, our traditions are all crumbling before our eyes. You've been absent from the everyday life that goes on out there for quite a while. Nothing is the same as before. Instead of those sad and joyous truths you described so poetically, we hear nothing but the screeching of the hyenas of the regime and the ravenlike cawing of the Zainab Sisters on every street corner."

I listened with my head drooping, downcast.

"As if all these afflictions were not enough," Bahaador went on, "the war with Iraq that started a few weeks ago has completely changed the course of events to the benefit of the mollahs. Using war propaganda, they are entrenching themselves deeper in this land. Instead of joyful laughter in the streets, lanes and market places you hear mourning and the wailing of fathers, mothers, sisters, and wives whose menfolk have been mutilated or killed in the war. The only things that are not affected by these calamities are Mount Damaavand and the Alborz Mountains, which are mutely witnessing yet more disasters. Maybe future generations will listen, as we do, to their murmurings and think of us, who, filled with naïve optimism, ran after that mirage of happiness and found nothing. Like little kids who go for the first time in their lives to the bazaar, we became very excited to see all those magical things. On the way home, however, our hopes of playing with our new toys were dashed as thieves beat us up, snatched them from us and ran off."

"You're right," I agreed. "I feel like one of those kids these days. How foolishly optimistic we all were when the whole nation rose against the Shah. How tirelessly we worked to help maintain that spring of freedom forever."

"Yes, mate," Bahaador said. "How hard we worked."

"Do you recall those days around the university?"

"How can I forget, Behrouz? I was there every day, attending endless meetings, sit-ins, and witnessing events in and around the place."

"The anarchic freedom was so magnificent to watch, wasn't it?" I said. "I often strolled among the throng gathered there to see what was going on. People from all sections of Tehran society and of all ages, women, men, and enthusiastic young people gathered there to sell all sorts of intellectual products without being hassled or bludgeoned by anyone. The massive railings around the university were covered with pictures of famous revolutionaries, ayatollahs, great statesmen, past and present intellectuals, and colourful slogans. The pavements were littered with piles of books and magazines – Marxist-Leninist reviews, books on politics, books on Islam, prayers books, revolutionary novels, comics, books on how to interpret the Koran, history books, all the books that were formerly banned under the Shah's regime. Every ten steps a young man or a woman stood on a wooden box, delivering a passionate speech on all manner of topical subjects such as the Islamic hijab, political economy, freedom of press, and how to prove the existence of God!"

"Many young boys and girls were handing out all types of political pamphlets to the drivers," Bahaador added.

"Mingled among this motley multitude was the army of street pedlars, hawkers, and stallholders who had never been anywhere near the university during the reign of the Pahlavis. Being astute business folk, they were quick to find the perfect opportunity to sell their wares," I said with a chuckle.

"Yes," Bahaador said, smiling. "I remember them clearly. They were freely expressing their opinions about politics for the first time in their lives."

"What I found hilarious," I said, "was that they spiced up their views about events at the time of the Shah with praise for their goods in order to sell as much as possible.

"They even strolled freely into the university, sat in some lectures, listened politely, and expressed their views. When out of the university, they began to repeat, somewhat parrot-fashion, what they'd learned to their customers and curious bystanders."

"Talking of them preaching to the onlookers," Bahaador said, "I couldn't help thinking of Fatmeh Cheragh-Ali. Do you remember that old woman?"

"How can I forget such a formidable old hag?" I said, smiling. "Every single day she would perch on a wooden fruit box placed just beside the main entrance of the university and croak loudly and passionately, like an old raven, praising Imam Khomeini and his henchmen."

"She just made me laugh so much the way she tucked her chador round herself, tying it behind her neck to free her clawlike hands which she frantically waved about in the manner of a demagogue," Bahaador reminisced.

"How the regime relied on poor, illiterate imbeciles like Fatmeh Cheragh-Ali to establish its illegitimate rule over the people."

"That's how they've stayed around so far, and I don't see any sign of them buggering off just yet."

"But, despite everything, those days were glorious, Bahaador," I said. "For the first time since the opening of the University of Tehran the barriers between the ivory-tower intellectuals and the masses had broken down. Everybody talked to everybody else without fear of being mocked, without showing off or feeling inferior. Professors, lecturers, doctors, artists, writers, and poets mingled among the hawkers, vendors, pedlars, day labourers, and soldiers, debating with them."

"Yes, that was exactly what was happening."

"As the joyful festive atmosphere carried on," I said, remembering some more amusing events, "several street entertainers joined in the show, mimicking the Shah's last speech before he fled, imitating some famous actors and actresses, dancing to the tune of popular street ditties that blared out from tape-recorders, singing revolutionary anthems, and even imitating some of those mollahs who licked the arses of the Shah and his cronies. This is what I call a real, genuine carnival as happened in ancient times. Oh, how much I enjoyed those days of short-lived, absolute anarchy. "

"Yes, mate," Bahaador agreed. "It was, alas, short-lived."

"Just like all of our happy times in this cursed land," I said. "Very soon gangs of bearded thugs, the devil knows from what shitholes they sprang, started to attack everybody who criticised Islam or expressed their views freely. These self-proclaimed *Hezbollahis* soon put a brutal end to the carnival atmosphere. Fed up with being beaten up, sworn at, or accused of being spies for America and Israel, the booksellers whose books were deemed to be dangerous for the regime packed up and went underground. The street entertainers, pedlars, and hawkers being by nature opportunistic, who don't give a damn about profound social changes, packed up their wares and carted them off to other, more promising, districts of Tehran such as around the Bazaar or more upmarket Tajrish Square."

The clamour outside was now deafening.

"You see, Bahaador," I said, "it would be unmanly and treacherous of me to save my skin by fleeing to another country, abandoning my friends in the trenches."

"How can you talk of friends, Behrouz?" Bahaador said. "Most of them are in prison, in hiding like you, maybe executed. Some have fled the country, and the ones who remain are either collaborating with the regime or keeping their mouths shut. Since you've been in hiding the world has moved on in a most frightening direction. The old order is crumbling about us so rapidly that we don't even have time to make sense of it all."

"I still want to stay," I repeated. "I cannot go on living outside my homeland."

"If you stay, Behrouz, they'll ferret you out and kill you in a matter of days and no one will even notice your disappearance. You'll either be poisoned in prison or battered to death by hatchet men in a vacant lot under cover of darkness. Your body will then be dumped somewhere on the outskirts of Tehran or thrown into the salt lakes in the middle of the desert." Bahaador clamped his lips closed and stared at me.

I realised how helpless I was. I no longer had the luxury of choice. Fate had clasped me in its deadly clutches, like a nasty little child who grabs a ragdoll by the throat and knocks it around, and will not let go till he has torn it into pieces. I had to make up my mind soon.

"What's to be done, then?" I asked reluctantly.

"We've arranged with some people smugglers to take you to the Pakistan border," Bahaador explained calmly. "From there, their contacts will take you to the United Nations Headquarters in Islamabad. Once with them, they will arrange a visa for you to go to one of the European countries. We don't know which one. Anywhere in this world is better than this shithole of a homeland for you."

I didn't know what to say. Outside, the daily hustle and bustle of the street traders, stallholders and hawkers was beginning to fill up the street down below. I thought with affection about those ordinary, hard-working, funny men and women, who, day in, day out, carted their wares around to make a living to support their families, whatever the social and political condition. They gave me a sense of something permanent to hold on to, something immortal. They had something unbreakable and lasting about them, these people who march on, despite all the odds against them. They are the real and omnipresent witnesses in the streets, lanes, squares, bazaars and market places who keep an eye on those whoresons in power. They carry on with their daily toils with colossal fortitude, secretly sharpening their daggers for the day of revenge. These souls are real survivors because they're shrewd, adaptable, and, above all, have a great sense of humour. They laugh, when joking among themselves, at those pompous men in power whose days of delusional glory are brief before they are kicked out of their thrones and castles. These clowns in power do not realise that whoever you are, wherever you spring from, whatever diamond-studded throne you sit on, you still sit on your arse, just like everybody else. March on, my real brothers, sisters, and mates. I salute you and wish you good luck.

The rabble in the employment of the regime down there was getting ready for the gruesome everyday carnival of hatred.

Bahaador told me he would come back with another friend late in the evening to whisk me away. He then left me alone again with a multitude of thoughts and images hitting themselves against my skull like demented lunatics. My whole life had been thrown into chaos. All my plans for the future, the plays, stories, and novels I was going to write, to play an active role in bringing about, however minuscule, meaningful cultural change, were all now a tangled confusion. I had never been outside my homeland. I had a minimal knowledge of the English language as we had been taught in the regime-controlled high schools. What was I supposed to do in an alien land without my family and friends? How would I settle down? What would I do to make a living? Would I be able to write and make plays? I would certainly not be able to write in English.

I perched on the workbench and held my head in my hands, overwhelmed by all these vague images of the future without my family and friends. I never, ever imagined in my wildest dreams that it would come to this. We had played an active role in our efforts to bring about some semblance of change to our plagued land. We did not know that it would end like this. It's true that revolutions, sooner or later, start devouring their own children. Why do we keep failing every time we have a revolution? Why do we have so many heroes who sacrifice so much for this nation? Why do they all end up being assassinated, tortured, forced to commit suicide or banished to foreign lands? Question after question crashed against the walls of my skull like dark waves. When were we going to wake up from our idle slumber? When were we going to join modern times? Why were we stuck like donkeys on treadmills in the remote villages, eternally going round and round, rolling the millstone, never breaking out of this vicious circle of stupidity and superstitions?

Next morning before daybreak Bahaador walked into the workshop carrying a large bundle.

"Come on, Behrouz," he said, fishing out a razor from the bag. "You must shave your face and moustache once again as clean as possible."

After making sure the blinds were completely shut, Bahaador asked me to stand in the far corner of the workshop and shave my face.

"How am I supposed to shave without hot water and soap?" I asked.

"I've brought a flask of hot water and a lump of soap," he said, handing me the soap and the flask. "I'll light my lighter to make sure you shave as best you can."

Careful not to cut my skin, I did a fairly good job.

"How does it look?" I asked Bahaador's opinion.

"It feels now as smooth as baby's bottom," he said, touching my face.

"All right then. I'm ready."

"Not yet."

"What do you mean?"

"We've to disguise you this time so that no one can recognise you."

"Without my bushy moustache and thick hair I look like a totally different person."

"I know you do," Bahaador said. "These bastards do not trust anyone and anything now. As they know that some people have fled in different disguises, they're even more cautious, sniffing everybody like mongrel dogs."

"What else can be done to my face, I wonder."

"Your face is pretty as it is," Bahaador said with a chuckle. "It'll be even prettier when you're veiled in a black chador."

"Black chador!" I let out a muffled cry.

"Yes, mate. A full-size black chador will do the job nicely."

"But I can't wear a frigging chador," I protested. "What will people think of me if they recognise me?"

"The only people who know who you are are me and the smugglers, that's all," Bahaador reassured me. "The police and the regime's henchmen in the streets see only a good Muslim sister very well wrapped up in her Islamic hijab."

Bahaador pulled a black chador out of the bag, handed it over to me and told me to put it on. I threw it over my bald head, covering it well, tightly pinching the two hems under my chin.

In the gleam of the lighter he peered into my face, looking satisfied.

"Hmm, now you look like one of those ugly Zainab Sisters," he said with a muffled laugh. "No one can imagine that a famous hunted man is hiding under that chador, Behrouz. "By the way, in case anybody asks you a question, try to answer in a feminine, coquettish voice."

"Thanks, mate," I replied. "I'll do my best. Only I should be careful not to act too flirty, otherwise those bastards might fancy me and create more unwished-for troubles."

Outside the block, one of those taxis that travel long distances all over Iran was waiting for us. Bahaador and I sat on the back seat pretending we were a married couple. Once we were settled, the driver, a bearded, rough-looking fellow with a keffiyeh round his neck, no doubt one of the smugglers, looked around and drove off, speeding through streets. After giving me instructions in his throaty voice, the morose-looking man remained quiet. He stopped the car in a deserted street. A bearded man, also wearing a keffiyeh, got into the car and sat in the front seat as mute as a dumb beast.

"All right, Behrouz," Bahaador said, looking at me, "this is the end of the line for me. These brothers will take you to the Pakistan border and pass you on to their friends there."

Bahaador gave me a hug, wished me good luck, and got out of the car. As the driver drove off I turned and looked at him standing alone and forlorn under the pale street lamp, wiping his tears. I hoped he would not be in any danger for doing so much for me. I didn't even have a chance to say goodbye to my wife. It would have been too dangerous. They told me as soon as I settled down somewhere she might be able to join me. I hoped they were right. The smugglers explained to me what to say and do in case we were stopped by the police or the Revolutionary Guards. They assured me that things would be all right as the country had been thrown into chaos due to the outbreak of the war with Iraq. They then kept silent, professionals who had been doing this kind of job for a long time.

The car drove through different districts of Tehran, which was beginning to stir in the smoggy light. Instead of seeing the present city, I saw images rising up from the dust and rubble of past years, the years of my childhood in downtown Tehran. In one familiar street I saw myself perched on my father's rickety bicycle, riding towards my first school. In the next street I saw the line of schoolchildren from my second school walking along the pavements to return home after school. In front of each alleyway one or two children darted out of line and disappeared into the lanes. I saw my very young self sauntering along to go to the baker's and grocer's first thing in the morning to buy freshly-baked bread, a lump of cheese, or butter, for the family's breakfast. When the car passed in front of a lane I saw my childhood friends running after a deflated plastic ball, kicking up a racket. Instead of seeing deserted, gloomy lanes, I saw street pedlars and hawkers hauling around their goods piled on donkeys, on carts or in large trays on their heads, singing loudly to announce their presence.

As the car passed through the Lalezaar district I saw my younger brother and myself scampering among the milling crowd, stopping in front of each cinema, and eagerly inspecting the pictures. I followed us as we stood in front of a cinema showing a Western film. Once we decided to see that film we fished out whatever pocket money we had in our pockets to see if we had enough to watch another film that day. Putting all our coins together, we decided to see the movie. After buying our tickets, roasted watermelon seeds, and *pirozhkies*, we vanished into the cinema.

Around Lalezaar-No, I recognised my mother among the throng of shoppers. Veiled in her colourful chador, she was skilfully manoeuvring her way through the crowd, haggling with this pedlar or that hawker to buy clothes for her small children. I saw all my small sisters and brother who, behaving sensibly, were quietly trailing behind her, holding each other's hands in order not to get lost in that bedlam of chanting, street songs pouring out of tape-recorders and non-stop brawls. As the car passed across the main Train Station Square, I saw my entire family huddled together in the middle of that vast station hall, waiting patiently to catch our first ever train to the Holy city of Mashhad. They all looked bewildered, seeing so many people rushing here and there to catch their trains to different parts of the country.

As the car moved on to unfamiliar districts, all those images slowly faded away, returning to the ruins of the past, turning into wandering phantoms who inhabited the realms belonging from now on only to the past where they truly belonged. What is this most mysterious thing we call *past* in our lives? Nothing will remain of my own childhood self and these dearest of all people whom I was going to leave behind but a cloud of thick dust raised as if by a magnificent horse galloping towards far-distant horizons.

Well-wrapped in my chador, I watched the desolate, quiet lanes on the southern outskirts of Tehran. This part of Tehran seemed like a huge, sprawling ruin after an earthquake. The new prevailing culture of terror had cast a black *abaa* over the lanes and alleyways, under which the terrified people smothered their sorrows about the dead and disappeared. Temporary shrines, garishly decorated with colourful lightbulbs, large photos of young souls killed at the front and Koranic verses stood at the entrance of many lanes. Gathered around these shrines were women, old and young, veiled in black chadors, which they clutched around them, mutely weeping for their departed sons or husbands. What a waste of young lives, I thought.

As the car left the city behind, I turned and looked back at the vast Behesht-e Zahra cemetery, beyond which stretched that monstrous capital city. I saw not a homeland, but a wasteland, shrouded in the sickly mist of a grey January day. On this land, forgotten by time and the rest of the humanity, nothing grew but thorns and bracken, among which crept and crawled the nastiest of creatures, crowned with black turbans and draped in camelhair *abaas*, resembling the dung-beetles and cockroaches that crawled out of holes, scuttled around for filth to feed upon, and crept into others.

Soon I am going to join the hordes of uprooted Iranians, wandering as homeless and hopeless as vagabonds, somewhere on this planet, I thought. In order to avoid any possible interrogation by the Revolutionary Guards and the police patrol, the smugglers parked the car in some place in the middle of nowhere. Having smuggled so many souls, they had thought of everything.

We passed through the border without any serious mishap as the sergeant in charge let us through. His palms had, no doubt, been greased beforehand. Once in Pakistan, I was handed over to two other accomplices, who drove me up and down many uninhabited mountain tracks. I was then given an Afghani-type burka that covered my face and entire body. As many of the tracks ran through mountains and valleys, we had to ride on donkeys and mules.

Finally, my adventures came to an end when we arrived at Islamabad. A Pakistani human rights activist who worked for Amnesty International took me straight to the office of two French human rights lawyers. They speedily got a visa for me and I soon found myself in Paris.

*

Brutally driven out of my homeland against my will and far away from the habits and norms I once accepted unquestioningly, here in this cold, gloomy city, my endless questing about my life began. Like those Furies in Greek mythology, the most painful questions and anxieties relentlessly assailed me, at all hours of the day.

The first year in exile was a hellish torment. Some of my friends who had left Iran before me were kind enough to accommodate me for a while. I had to move constantly from one home to another for fear of my life as the assassins of the regime were hard at work to find me. They had already killed a large number of political activists and poets inside and outside Iran. I found it hard and painful to adjust to this unsettling life of vagrancy and exile. Feelings of guilt that I had escaped like a coward, leaving my family and friends behind, a sense of absolute helplessness, plagued my waking and sleeping hours. I was terrified to be on my own, constantly seeking the company of the other exiles who were even more wretched than I was. Like a fearful brotherhood of lepers, we haunted dingy little coffee shops, old Iranian restaurants, to huddle together in a corner and tell the tales of our ruined lives and hopes. We attended political and social meetings to talk endlessly about how to play our, albeit insignificant, role in bringing about some change, however little, to our plagued land.

Late at night, once we left our haunts and those noisy gatherings that gave us the illusion of togetherness and a sense of belonging, we scurried, each on our own in the dark, misty streets of Paris, hugging the walls, constantly glancing over our shoulders in case an assassin would leap out of the shadows and put an end to our wretched existence. We had to take refuge in our tomb-like little flats as soon as possible. I never, ever found anything romantic about this city. It never crossed my mind to go to all those museums, galleries, cathedrals, and parks to distract myself and learn something about my host country. None of my friends even suggested to me to visit such places. How could these alien cultural places console the broken soul of an exile? A mind plagued with life and death worries, a mind preoccupied with the most painful existential questions can never be a culture-vulture, gallivanting from one museum or gallery to another in the futile hope of distracting itself. Even walking in the streets during the day among those total strangers, who spoke a language that I did not understand, was a nightmare that happened in open daylight. I felt I was like an invisible being, a ghost who walked among the living, who belonged to their homeland, talked and laughed, going about their daily lives, who, at the end of the day, returned to their families and homes. These strangers did not even glance at me, and if they did, their glance was hostile and hateful.

As I had to write to drive my demons away, with the little money I was left with I rented a cheap flat in a rundown district of Paris. Every night I would write till the small hours, in Persian of course, whatever came to my mind – short stories, articles, plays, anything. Exhausted, like a horse who had galloped all night, I would then collapse on the bed. The moment I laid my head on the pillow the Furies, whom I had forced into temporary silence, would rise again and jeer at me, doing their best to drive me to despair and insanity, making me think of suicide, to put an end to my misery. I would fall into a shallow sleep, only to be assailed by frightening nightmares about scenes of my friends back in in Iran being tortured, shot at point blank range in the head, my wife and my family. I would sit up in bed, my head still full of sound and fury, light a cigarette, and peer into darkness like someone possessed. Realising that sleep would not bring any solace, I would sit at my table and write. When I read my stories later on in the day, they all sounded incoherent, with a nightmarish quality, devoid of any sense of humour like the ones I used to write years ago in my homeland.

Even when my wife, with the help of human smugglers, joined me, I went on for a long time fighting my demons. I wrote numerous articles, short stories, and plays in fledgling Iranian journals for which I earned some measly cash. In the first few years the Iranian exiles were very active, living in false hope that if they wrote and took part in demonstrations and attended endless meetings, soon the regime in Iran would collapse and everyone would go back and live happily ever after.

Disenchanted, year after year many poets, writers, and artists were either assassinated by the agents of the regime inside and outside Iran, or died due to loneliness and heartache. Despite all odds, I and a small number of my friends carried on writing and publishing in numerous journals. After a few years, however, the enthusiasm of most of my companions slowly dried up, because of the worsening situation in Iran. Weighed down by money worries and despair, some of them emigrated to more promising climes, others found jobs in universities and other institutions, and as time wore on, they forgot all about their ideals and hopes for the future of their homeland. Many of them are now married with kids of their own, leading quiet lives in different parts of this planet.

I, however, am not one who abandoned my ideals. The tough and painful experience of exile had been similar to that of a furnace in which the rich ore is heated to extract the precious metal. All the impurities are burnt now, leaving nothing but that core of my being of which only I and no one else knows its value. Those bastard mollahs with their rotten, archaic religion represent death, and I represent life.

O life! I will go on forging in the smithy of my mind the untold tales of my people.

Glossary

abaa: a coarse fabric of wool or hair fibre with a felted finish worn over other clothing by the Islamic clergy in Iran.

agha: means Mr or sir. The word is often used as a courtesy before a man's name to show respect.

allaameh: an honorific title given to an erudite man

arrack: a distilled alcoholic drink

astaghforellah: Allah forgive me

aye zeki: an expression of surprise mixed with mockery

babaa: literally means 'father'. But it is used as a word of endearment when an older person addresses a younger person or one who does not see sense.

baleh: yes

basiji: a member of the paramilitary volunteer militia, *basij*, established after the Islamic Revolution. The basij receive their orders from and are subordinate to the Revolutionary Guards.

binekaah: an Arabic term for an unmarried woman

chador: literally means 'tent'. An open black cloak or veil that covers the head and the entire body.

divan: collected work of a poet

efreeteh: a female evil spirit or powerful demon in Arabian-Islamic mythology

Esfehani: a native of the city of Esfehan

Ey baba: Ey means O! Oh! as in Oh God! *Ey baba* is an expletive to express a sense of surprise or resignation about something.

Farvardin: the first month of the Iranian solar calendar (31days) corresponding roughly to April

ghabaa: a long shirt for men, open in front and without a collar, still worn in some rural parts of Iran

ghazal: Arabic and Iranian poetry composed in repeating rhymes that deals with love, betrayal, the pain of loss and separation, simple pleasures of life such as wine, appreciation of beauty of all kinds and companionship

ghelman: according to the Koran, ghelmans are pretty young men who will be the companions of devout Muslim women in paradise

hadith: the body of the transmitted actions and sayings of the Prophet Mohammad and his companions

Haaj Agha: this expression combines the title of *haaji* (a Muslim who has completed the pilgrimage to Mecca and therefore been given this honorific title) with that *agha* to convey respect to the person – often a cleric, or someone in a position of authority, or more commonly simply a man who is older. (Men are often called *haaj agha* out of respect without having ever actually made the pilgrimage.)

Haft-Sin: a table arrangement of seven symbolic items traditionally displayed at *Nowruz*. The haft-sin table includes seven items all starting with the letter sin in the Persian alphabet.

hammaam: a public bathhouse

Hazrat: his holiness

Hezbollahi: a member of the *Hezbollah* (Party of Allah) formed by Khomeini after the Islamic Revolution

Hojjat-ol-eslam: the title of a cleric who has completed his theological studies

Hojjat-ol-eslam-e-val-moslemin: a mollah who has much higher rank than *hojjat-ol-eslam*

houri: according to the Koran, a beautiful young virgin lady who takes care of Muslim men in paradise

inshallah: god willing

jaan: dear

jenaab: an honorific title for men, excellency

kharposhteh: a small attic-like room that opens out on to a roof

korsi: a traditional system of heating in the colder regions of Iran, and some other countries. It is made up of a hot charcoals in a brazier placed under a large, wooden, square-shaped, low table covered with a large quilt. Members of a family slip, in ones or twos, under the quilt on each side of the table.

laa elaaha ellallah: there is no God but Allah

Mash: *mash* is a simplified and familiar form for *Mashhadi* that is an honorific title for someone who has been on a pilgrimage to the shrine of Imam Reza in Mashhad.

mashallah: an Arabic phrase that expresses appreciation, joy, praise, or thankfulness for an event or person that was just mentioned. While mashallah is used as an expression of respect, it also serves as a reminder that all accomplishments are considered by Muslims to be achieved through the will of Allah. It is generally said upon hearing good news.

Mir: short form of *emir* that means a Muslim ruler, commander, or prince

Monkaraat: Vice Squad

muezzin: a person who calls Muslims to prayer (usually from the minaret of a mosque)

Moharram: is the first month of the Islamic calendar. It is one of the four sacred months of the year. On the tenth day of this month Shiite Muslims commemorate the martyrdom of Imam Hossein, the grandson of Prophet Mohammad, fourteen centuries ago.

morshed: in this case the puppet-master

Nakir and Monker: according to Islamic tradition, these are the angels, Nakir and Monker, who question a person in the grave. They visit the tombs of those who have recently died. They are to determine where the deceased will go, to Paradise or to Hell. They ask questions regarding the religious beliefs of the individual, and also their good and evil deeds on earth. The good are shown what life will be like in Heaven. The bad are shown the torments of Hell.

namaaz: Persian term for prayers, Islamic or non-Islamic

naneh: in Azeri Turkish it means mamma or ma. Sometimes people call any old lady *naneh* out of respect that means grandmother or granny.

Nowruz: Nowruz, meaning literally 'The New Day', is the Iranian New Year celebrated on the first day of Farvardin (21 March).

ostaad: master, master craftsman

paadeshah: a/the king, the monarch, the sovereign, the shah *pirozhi*: Russian dumplings

Rostam: the greatest hero of pre-Islamic Persian legend of Ferdowsi's epic poem called Shahnameh (the tenth-century Book of Kings)

Salaam: greeting, hello

Salaam aleikom: the formal greeting of all Muslims, meaning 'Peace be upon you'

samaa: the Sufi ritual of chanting and dancing

sangak bread: a type of Iranian bread baked on hot pebbles

SAVAK: the infernal secret police of the Pahlavi Regime

SAVAKi: a member of SAVAK

sayyed: an honorific title denoting males accepted as descendants of the Islamic Prophet
Muhammad

Shahr-e No: literally 'The Citadel of the New City'. It was the largest brothel in Iran, enclosed by a wall. Reza Shah ordered the building of this Citadel so that all the prostitutes would conduct their business in one place instead of being scattered all over Tehran.

shahi: a small coin of the late Qajar period

siegheh: under Shiite Law a man may have a maximum of four wives. In addition he's allowed an unlimited number of temporary wives, who make a marriage contract for a period ranging anywhere from one hour to ninety-nine years. These siegheh wives have no inheritance rights and are not officially registered with the city or the mosque.

taftoon bread: a type of round flat bread popular in central Iran

ta'zieh: Persian version of Islamic opera re-enacting the death of martyrs who were killed in Karbala along with Imam Hussein during the month of Moharram

tekieh: a temporary mosque made chiefly to commemorate the Shiite festivals of Ashura when Imam Hossein and his kin were martyred in Karbala fourteen centuries ago

tiarte: a distorted term for theatre used by common people

toman: an unofficial monetary unit in Iran, equal to ten rials

vallah: by God

yallah: go, get going

Zainab: the granddaughter of the Islamic Prophet, Mohammad, who took part in the battle of Karbala alongside her brother, Imam Hossein

Biography

Feridon Rashidi was born in Iran in 1955 and came to the UK in 1977. Resident in London, for 29 years he taught in several primary schools in the city. With five degrees from two London University Colleges (B.Sc. Psychology, B.A. French Language and Literature, PGCE, M.Sc. in Child Development, and MA in Theory and Practice of Translation from French to English) he is fluent in Farsi and French. He is now a full-time writer and has written more than 32 short stories, 25 of which are published as a collection, *Tales of Iran*, including the prize-winning stories, *Ashura* and *The Pigeon-fancier* that are published on *writers'hub.com, Iranian.com,* and *Mechanics' Institute Review (MIR online).* He has also published a novel, *The Outcast*.

Lightning Source UK Ltd.
Milton Keynes UK
UKOW04f1817260717
306110UK00001B/151/P